WAKING SLOW

IOANNA OPIDEE

Waking Slow
Ioanna Opidee

PFP INC
publisher@pfppublishing.com
PO Box 829 Byfield, MA 01922

Printed in the United States of America
© 2018 Ioanna Opidee

ISBN-13: 978-1-7324322-0-8

Front Cover Painting:
Girl on Window
© Jelena Marinkovic
Image used by kind permission of the artist

For my daughters, Joni and Mary

Acknowledgements

The opportunity to express my gratitude for the many people who have helped to shape and nurture this work is a gift. I thank you for reading.

Many thanks are due to Peter Sarno, a generous spirit who serves as a bulwark of the literary arts, who believed in this project enough to bring it to light, and who connected me with Martha Carlson-Bradley, who edited these pages with care, compassion, and clarity.

Thanks, also, to Michael White for linking me with the many writers and teachers in Fairfield University's Low Residency MFA Program who taught me how to call myself a writer: my mentors, Lary Bloom, Roya Hakakian, and Kim Kupperman; Rachel Basch, who read an early draft of this novel and offered invaluable insight and good faith; Da Chen, whose boundless energy gave fuel to the writing of this story; and Baron Wormser, who first suggested I try writing fiction. To my many friends and fellow writers in the community: Daisy Abreu, Chris Belden, Alena Dillon, David Fitzpatrick, Elizabeth Hilts, Nalini Jones, and A.J. O'Connell, who knew and cared for a nascent version of Rinie; my fellow essayists and writing buddies, Jamie Chesbro and Brian Hoover; and Sonya Huber, whose infectious momentum carries the community forward. To Cinthia Gannett, a true mentor, and to Lisa Bankoff, for her guidance and encouragement. To Ravi Shankar, for publishing a version of some of this material in

Drunken Boat. To Rob Cotto, who lent his market expertise early on, and John Whaley, who offered his critical acumen late in the game. To Pamela Annas at the University of Massachusetts Boston, and to Askold Melnyczuk, whose workshop introduced me to Peter Sarno and who encouraged me to be fearless in my writing. To Mrs. Rita Green, who introduced me to the poetry of Theodore Roethke. And to the many other teachers, friends, and fellow writers who are too innumerable to list here...please know that I appreciate you a great deal.

Thank you, also, to my students—all of them, past and present—for teaching and challenging me to articulate with greater clarity and impact.

To my mother and father, who have always believed that I have something to say, and selflessly gave me every opportunity to figure out how to say it.

To my sisters, nephews, niece, and family-in-law, whose love means the world.

To my daughters, Joni and Mary, who are precious beyond words.

And to my beloved husband, Eric, who supports whatever I choose to do or be; who I know will love me just as much if I write ten more books or none at all.

I honor the privilege of saying, *thank you.*

"We think by feeling. What is there to know?"
-*Theodore Roethke, "The Waking"*

"But to enjoy freedom . . .
we have of course to control ourselves."
-*Virginia Woolf*

CHAPTER ONE
THE MORNING AFTER

I wake to find an arm across my chest. I turn to look beside me and see Andy.

I make a motion to get up, but the arm holds me down, like the bar in a roller coaster car.

"Where you going?" His eyes are still shut; his free hand, palm up, is over his forehead.

"I have to go," I say, my voice too hurried, too faint, too breathless. My body feels wispy and fine, like a thistle in the wind.

"Why?" He half-opens one eye and angles it toward me.

My mind sifts through possible reasons and plucks out the sharpest one: "My mom is coming to visit."

The air here is thick, dank, cold, and salted with sweat. The walls are a pale, putrid yellow like jaundiced fingernails and bare— except for the poster of a woman in a bright orange thong, bending over a shallow wave.

"Why?" he repeats, the arm still firm.

I feign the first half of a laugh. "We're going shopping."

He peers at me through narrowed eyes. "You're lying. You're not going shopping."

And he's right. I am lying.

"You're not going anywhere." The arm presses down harder now. "You're staying here."

So I wait for a few beats of time until he dozes back into languor, then try again, lifting my torso up from the gray jersey sheets that are hot against my back.

1

"Where you going?" he repeats, this time with both eyes open and set on my face, his upper body raised to a half-sit. The pressure from the arm eases a bit, but the words now, their tone, are what hold me in place.

I release a giggle, that ever-female sound, a shield against the tension, and it suffocates me. But I manage to say, "I told you. I have to meet my mom." And then I add, "I don't want her to wonder where I am."

The arm gives way further now as I push against it. I climb over his body and hop to the floor, while his head falls back to the pillow, resigned.

Facing the door, I reach for my jeans, rumpled in a heap beside the extra-long twin bed. I'm careful not to glance back as I dress, and as I creak open the bedroom door, then tiptoe down the hall to the bathroom he shares with three room-mates.

On tiptoe, as if treading so lightly could make me not there.

In the bathroom, I sidestep a crumpled magazine face open to the image of a naked woman clutching her breasts as she straddles the back of a chair; at the sink, sprinkled with tiny black hairs like eyelashes, I set aside a topless stick of deodor-ant swimming in the basin and grab the near-empty tube of toothpaste that is tucked behind the faucet. I squeeze a pea-sized drop from the curled-up plastic onto my forefinger and press it down into the ridges of my teeth, the flesh of my gums, feeling primitive and like a thief. The only towel in sight—used and frayed—sags wet across the tilted shower curtain rod, so I splash my face with cold water and dry my hands on my hair.

With my bag strapped across my chest, I leave the bath-room and the dorm apartment, speed-walk down the hall and stairs, and push on the metal bar of the building's back door to fling it open. I relish the cold hard clink and its after-feel, step through the doorway and inhale deeply—gasping for that crisp

New England air.

I stand with my back to Andy's dorm building. It feels early, very early—the air has a thick, fog-like stillness to it, like the opening screenshot in a film where only the sky and treetops are in view before the camera pans down to ground level: to a quiet, dusty parking lot packed with unmoving cars, the brilliant green of a silent football field in the distance; crushed beer cans strewn at the foot of a concrete garbage container, the putrid smell of vomit and alcohol emanating from its interior. Not a person in sight.

I close my eyes, then open them again, electrified, like a bug in a zapper, I walk forward through the empty campus, past the neighboring dorm building and the dining hall, where the scent of laundry wafts through a shiny metal vent. I continue up the hill to the front gate of campus, and over toward the T stop. All the while it feels as though I've stepped into a bubble that is rolling along the ground, filled with a viscous, pulsating matter.

The T isn't there when I reach the station, so I head down Commonwealth Avenue toward the next stop. Again, the train isn't there, but I cannot, will not, cannot stop to wait, so I continue walking, toward the next station, and the next, until I abandon the train all together because the *moving forward* feels too good.

I walk straight for miles until I reach Mass Ave, where I turn left toward the Harvard Bridge that crosses the Charles River. Finally, I stop on the pedestrian pathway and lean hard against a railing. The water below seems to pull at me, beckoning as if it promises to catch me if I jumped.

After a while, I head back toward the tip of Newbury Street, to the Urban Outfitters store. It's past 9:00 a.m. by now, the air has grown warmer, and the shop appears to be open. I pause for a moment before treading into the store, feeling welcomed by its grandness, its sparkling chandelier, its two-story ceiling and staircase. The air conditioning knocks into me like a wave, and the room makes me feel—for the first time since stepping a foot outside of Andy's building—that I can breathe; it gives me space.

I climb the stairs to the second floor and drift through the meandering aisles of clothing racks and tables, the fingertips of my right hand extending and retracting, grazing fabrics at a regular interval—*touch, pause, touch, pause, touch*. Cotton, linen, silk, wool, cotton, wool, silk, linen, cotton, linen—no orderly pattern to the textures, only to the rhythm of my touching. Meanwhile, all around me: chatty girls hum on cell phones, salespeople offer assistance amid funkily-dressed mannequins, towers of multi-colored cashmere, piles of handbags, and a wall display of slip-on shoes. The bubble around my body throbs and zaps, a force field gaining strength in every moment I spend in the store.

"Can I help you with something?" A salesgirl appears beside me, wearing cowboy boots, denim shorts, and a green-and-white-striped shirt that hangs off one shoulder.

Help me? Can she?

I smile and say, "No, thank you. Just looking."

My fingers, now, hold tightly to a thin piece of silken material—a sash. The salesgirl sings, "Okay, let me know if I can!" and struts onward.

I watch her go, then look closely at the sash, its swirling patterns of purple and black. *I like this*, I think and wrap it around my waist. *I can wear this as a belt. Now that would jazz me up.* I finger the price tag—seven dollars. Too much for a piece of fabric. So I return it to its metal hook.

But after making yet another lap around the store, I find myself returning—like a whole new person—to the table with the sash, and I slip the item out from the pile.

I want it; I don't want to buy it, but I want it.

I turn my hand and smooth the material with my thumb, then release my grip, letting loose the fabric. It falls into my shoulder bag as I caress a lambswool sweater with my other, free hand.

Easy.

For an instant, I don't move, in mock-consideration of the sweater, then glide on to the next exhibit, to peruse the earrings, necklaces, and hair clips splayed out on the table. My mind tunes only to the color and luster of each piece, instead of the item lying perilously within my purse.

Minutes later, I trek down the stairs and toward the door. By the time I push it open, I've forgotten the sash entirely—until the blaring *Errr, Errr, Errr,* of the store alarm invades my ears, my mind, the store . . . the entire city. I glance over my shoulder and see a young man—a few years older than me is my guess—stalking over to me, dressed in a black vest, a gray-and-white checkered shirt, tight jeans, and black-rimmed glasses.

"Can I see your bag?" he asks.

"I don't have a bag," I say. "I didn't buy anything."

"Your pocketbook, then. Can you open it for me?"

"Sure." Because what can I do? With shaky hands, I swivel my shoulder-bag to the front of my body and open it wide to reveal the contents. He reaches in and pulls out the sash, draped directly, unabashedly, on top.

"This is store merchandise," he says.

"Oh," I say, stung by my own abrasive falseness. "I don't know how it got in there. It must have dropped without me realizing—"

"I can have you arrested for this," he says with one hand on his hip, while the other hand rattles the sash. "You know that." He says this as a statement, as if he knows me, and what I should know.

"It was an accident," I say evenly. "I really don't know how it got in there. It must have fallen in while I was holding it."

He leers into my face, seeing every rotten thing I've ever done, and says, "I shouldn't let this go."

No, you shouldn't, says a voice in my head. My body holds its breath, to prepare, as if it might burst apart there in the lobby, or else evaporate and join the dust particles floating haplessly under the neon store lights.

"I'm sorry for the confusion," I say in a trembling voice that I loathe as much as he must.

Confusion. What confusion? I focus on the store manager name badge that hangs from his neck: *Lew.*

He glares at me with his dark eyebrows pinched. "Just go," he sighs. And then, like an older brother, he adds, "But don't ever do this again."

Shaking my head *no,* I backpedal out, then walk farther and farther away from all thoughts of the store and the sash, the alarm and Lew—his glasses and jeans and words and stares. I continue down Newbury, my line of vision fixed upward a bit from the standard eye level—to the space right above the average man's head, as if my own stare might sear a hole through somebody else's. The drumbeat of footsteps, the prattle of faceless voices, the sonorous hum of the car engines, the chiming *bring* of bicycle bells, the blaring police sirens, the entreating panhandlers—all become one composite sound, a jazz riff. Within minutes, I'm where I need to be—safe within a thoughtless mental space, the buzzing force field still surrounding my body, but now with an accompanying soundtrack.

I turn right onto Dartmouth Street and a wider, wall-less vista presents itself, dotted with flocks of moving people. A breeze now is trailing me—guiding me, or keeping vigil. No matter which one. I tilt my head upward to feel the sun hot on my face, extend my arms down and just a bit out at the sides so

I can press my palms against the wind, to feel its resistance and my own force pushing against it. When I come to the intersection of Dartmouth and Boylston, I wait for the road to clear, then tread diagonally across the four-way intersection, hopping the curb to Copley Square Plaza.

There, I see Trinity Church, with its dramatic archways, steeples, and spires, all a rich brown with tints of red that make them appear almost purple. Behind the church, the John Hancock building—a shiny, modern tower of glass.

Always reflecting what's outside, I think, *never within. All we want is to see ourselves in everything else.*

I move instead toward the sepia-toned church—a relic, out of place in this busy, bustling square. Gabriel, a freshman-year friend from Argentina, used to tell me stories of his summer wanderings through the city streets of Europe, where he slept in churches—where the churches don't lock up at night, he said; where they'll never turn anyone away.

I grasp the cold, iron handle of the towering mahogany door at the front entrance of the church and am surprised, despite what I know, that it gives way when I pull.

The narthex is silent, dimly lit, and still—startlingly still, unlike the commotion outside the doors. I pull a dollar from my wallet and drop it into the bin beside the candles, then slip out a thin taper and press it down into the sand, watching the grains part way for the wax.

Inside this quiet, motionless space, every moment is an eternity, with its own story—a beginning, middle, and end, as if whole lives could be lived in the space of an instant.

"Please, God, keep my family and friends safe, healthy, and happy," I whisper, a habit—the simplest prayer in my repertoire.

Two women—one elderly wearing a grandiose, magenta-colored hat, and the other middle-aged dressed in white pants and a blue blazer—light their candles. They offer me polite, warm smiles.

I smile in return, mechanically, like a creepy toy.

They move past and I whisper my prayers again, two more times to reach three, then make three signs of the cross, forcefully tapping my forehead and gut, my right shoulder then left, then I kiss the tips of my three pursed fingers before heading through the doorway to the nave. Greeted by a burst of hot, stale air, I take a seat in the third to last row and let out a sigh and a "Huh," as I realize how automatic it is, this counting of threes—Father, Son, and Holy Spirit—though, truth be told, I haven't prayed like this in years.

A few rows up, a little boy holding hands with his dad, turns to check for the source of the noise, and I smile, but his head whips back to face front. A minute later, when the dusty-haired boy and his dad move on, he glances over his shoulder as he's led away—still deciding on me, in that little boy way—and then I find myself alone.

This church is darker than I expected—everything deep burgundy or mahogany brown, and the ceiling as high as any I can recall. My eye is drawn to the whitest, brightest spot in the expansive space—the altar table. A cloth with the image of two peacocks looking away from one another drapes it. Atop are two large candles, above which hangs a large wooden cross. The cross itself is suspended by two chains extending from an emblem that features a white dove flying downward, with the sun, whose rays beam triumphantly outward, behind it.

It seems odd, this dove, flying downward, with such abandon. Isn't the dove a sign of peace? What's peaceful about that?

An inscription, placed high on the back wall of the church, states, *"Ye Shall Know the Truth and The Truth Shall Make You Free."*

I reread the lines in my mind a few times, waiting for something to happen.

Truth, I think. *Free . . .*

It sounds so right, so much like what I need.

To the left, another passage: *"He that Doeth the Will of God Abideth Forever."*

"Doeth the Will of God . . . ," I say aloud.

My voice echoes like breath in a jar. I gaze into the vault at the center of the ceiling and suppress the urge to cry.

I steady my line of vision onto the patterns in the vault, like I did every Sunday as a kid in my own church. The words inscribed along its base read *"Unto the Lamb Forever Blessing and Honour and Glory."*

The Lamb . . .

My mind flashes to Grandma. Can she see me up there? Did she see me today . . . and last night?

It's been two weeks since she died. It probably took her this long to make her way to Heaven, and now she's settled in and scanning down and thinking, "So this is what Miss Rinie's all about. This is what she does . . ."

I grip the oak of the pew. Time slows and I'm sucked into a beam of memory. Eight years old, at her mobile home in the next town over from ours, for a sleepover. Perched together on the blue tile steps leading up to the bathtub, waiting for the water to warm and fill it.

"So, Miss Rinie," she said, her fingers dangling beneath the faucet. "Do you like any boys at school?"

"No *way!*" I said quickly.

"No?"

I shook my head and shrugged, glancing sideways at her. "A boy likes me, though. At least that's what everyone says."

I hadn't told anyone in my family this. Liking boys, in my house, was not just forbidden but a cause for shame. Good girls didn't like boys, in Greek families; not until they were old enough to think about marriage.

But Grandma, my mother's mother, wasn't Greek. And she wasn't, I sensed—even as a little girl—the type to judge.

"Oh really?" she said sweetly. "And you don't like him back?"

"No *way!*" I said. "He's Richard Bosh! He chases me and my friends around the playground, and he's *weird!*"

Grandma's hands fell into her lap. "Irinie!" she said. "I'm surprised at you. You know that's not nice, calling people names."

"But it's *true!* He *is* weird. Everybody says so. He's the biggest kid in the class!"

"But Rinie, how do you think he *feels* when people call him that?"

I hadn't thought of that. To my classmates and me, he was more like a monster from *Scooby Doo* than a real kid like us. "But, he's Richard Bosh . . ." I said, increasingly aware of my own unawareness.

"Yes, and he's a *person.* With thoughts and feelings, just like you. How do you suppose it makes him *feel* when you call him weird?" she repeated.

"Well . . . I don't think I've actually *called* him weird. Other than just now . . ."

Grandma nodded and turned her attention to the water. "Maybe that's why he likes you." Eyes on the stream, her tone rose higher: "You should be a little nicer to him. His feelings must be hurt."

After that, I *was* nicer to Richard Bosh, even though it made him chase me around the playground all the more, and even though the other kids started chanting, "Rinie and Richie, sitting in a tree . . . ." Nothing could be worse than that teasing for a girl who wanted mostly to blend in. Nothing, that is, but doing *wrong.* Being *bad.*

It was the only time I could remember disappointing my grandmother, but I learned from it this: You must *always* consider the feelings of others. You must *always* do the right thing. You must *always* be kind—even to those who seem like monsters.

A burst of energy courses through me, as if I've been standing here in the pew trying to make a decision and have suddenly come to one, only I don't know exactly what that decision is—nor the original choice. I rise from my seat and shift out from the row, then leave the church. I walk back down Dartmouth, onto Newbury, and up the half mile or so it takes to reach the Urban Outfitters store. As soon as I enter, I see Lew standing behind the register. When I approach him, he tilts his head to the right, his forehead crinkling. Before he has a chance to speak—before I can even reach him—I blurt, "I lied to you earlier. You know that. I'd like to buy the sash, please."

With his pointer finger, he pushes up the glasses that have slipped down the bridge of his nose. "Excuse me?"

"I want to buy the sash. I know that won't make it right, but it's the least I can do."

"Listen," he says, and sighs. "This stuff happens all the time . . ."

I shake my head. "Not with me. Do you still have the sash? Can I buy it?"

He stares at me for a long beat of time, then shrugs and finally says, "Well, sure . . ."

He grabs the sash from the counter behind him, rings it up, and adds, "You know, I've never seen anybody come back like this. It's actually kind of admirable."

"Please," I say. "What I did was terrible, and coming back doesn't change that."

"Well, yeah, but it does happen all the time. The stealing, I mean." He stuffs the sash into the bag with the receipt. "I

11

mean, yeah, it's wrong. But it's a seven-dollar sash. And like I said, I've never seen anybody come back."

I shake my head and take the bag from his hands. "You're wrong about me. But thank you for letting me buy this."

An hour later, in my room, I switch on the computer and sign on to instant messenger. I haven't even sat down yet when a message pops up, from someone named *Andyboy12*. "Hi," the message reads.

It's him, I think, but write, "Hi. Who's this?"

"You forgot me already? It's Andy, from last night. Remember, you told me your screen-name?"

I did?

I rifle through my memory of the evening. *I did*. "Right. Yeah. I didn't think you'd remember, though." I sit, now, with legs folded on the bed, pull the keyboard onto my lap, and lean in closer to the screen.

"Of course I remembered," he writes. "I have an amazing memory." I inhale deeply and feel a brush of pity for him. That false arrogance again . . .

"Anyway," he continues. "I wanted to say that I'm sorry about what happened last night."

My hands shake as I read his words. There's a part of me that wants him to continue—to tell me what, precisely, he is sorry for—but another part of me wants him to stop. I don't want to think about last night.

My first impulse is to write, hastily, "It's okay," just to halt the whole situation. Or, because isn't that what you're supposed to do when someone says they're sorry? But the message box shows that he's still typing, and a braver, darker part of me wants to know what he could possibly say next.

"I've had a bad reputation in the past," he writes, "but I'm different now . . . Really."

Different how? A reputation for what? Among whom? *Who is this guy,* I wonder, *and what is he saying?* "I understand," I write—though, severely, I don't.

My pity for him grows. I imagine his remorse, awake and sober now and seeing more clearly what has happened. Part of me wants to make him feel better, to tell him, "It was my fault; I shouldn't have been in your bed," but I write instead, "It was a weird situation."

"Right," he writes in return. "It was."

"A misunderstanding, I guess," I can't stop myself from typing.

"Right."

"I mean, it was weird," I repeat—this, an effort not to dismiss this nagging feeling I have so quickly. *But he's apologizing. He feels bad.* "But I understand," I write again.

"Good, good," he responds.

There is silence on his end for a longer stretch of time, which makes me wonder if the conversation is over, or if there is something I need, now, to say. "Hey, maybe we can hang out again soon," he writes. "Party, have some drinks."

Party? Drinks?

"Sure," I write. *He's trying to be nice. Or maybe he likes me. Maybe he feels bad for how things started between us. Maybe he really is a good guy, and really does want . . .*

"Sounds good," I add.

"So, you're cool, then?"

"Yes, I'm cool."

"Cool! LOL."

The forcefield protecting my body dissipates. I collapse onto my bed and lie there until I fall asleep.

Chapter Two
Age Seven

As a child, I was fearless and believed in love; that I *was* love, maybe, or that I had enough of it inside me to heal, tame, protect. And so it seemed natural that Pappou chose me, one summer evening when I was seven, to take on a journey— "somewhere special," he'd said; on a *volta,* a Greek word I loved, which meant outing, stroll, *adventure.*

We'd arrived in the village of Rafti, on the island of Minos, a few hours earlier. My grandparents, Yiayia and Pappou, had prepared an elaborate feast for our arrival. Afterward, my older sisters, Eugenia and Vicky, piled on the couch with my aunt Thia Mina and Yiayia to gossip about boys and makeup and things I was too embarrassed to even listen to, while my mother unpacked, and my big brother, Mark, took the bus into town to see the friends he'd met the summer before. Meanwhile, I sat perched on the cement wall of the veranda, with an arm draped over the wrought-iron railing, admiring an elaborate structure on the peak of the mountain across the way, imagining myself on a trek toward it. It resembled a palace, with spiring fortress walls. Pappou sat nearby on a small wooden stool painted periwinkle blue, cracking almonds in silence and tossing the empty shells into a dirty bucket. I'd wanted to ask him about the palace, what it was and who lived there, even though Yiayia had already told me the year before that it was a monastery, the home of priests, but I thought I might hear it again, anew. His

14

silence, though, was firm and commanding, so I abided by it, until he puffed a wide ring of smoke from his Marlboro Red into the sky and announced that he wanted to take me somewhere.

"Where?" I chirped, hopping to my feet and brushing the hair out of my eyes.

"You'll see," he said. He pushed down on his legs with his scabby hands and lifted himself up with a grunt. "*Pamé*, let's go."

Together, we traipsed through the village along a narrow, winding path of stone and pebble, sidestepping lemons and lizards, crushing fallen figs, entranced into a quiet harmony by the scent of basil and jasmine, and the singing cicadas.

This footpath was familiar to me—we'd taken it earlier that day when we'd arrived; it was the only way through the village. And yet each detail looked as if it were out of a storybook. It seemed impossible that I was actually there. Only the night before, my father and I had sat lounging on our porch back in Rhode Island, just the two of us gazing up at the stars in the cool of a dark June night. He leaned back on a lawn chair, his slippered feet resting on the patio table glass, hands clasped behind his head, while I sat up on my knees and slurped a vanilla ice cream cone. "You can love a place and miss a place the way you love and miss a person," he'd told me. "Minos is your home, like Milton is your home. It is yours, like it is mine."

I didn't know why he was telling me this, except that I could see from the way he stared at the peak of the table umbrella instead of at me that he felt sad he wasn't coming; he had to stay behind to work at the family diner. "You'll remember that one day when I'm gone," he added.

Of course I hated when he said that, about being gone someday—I knew about death but didn't like it—so I ignored the comment. "But I'm only there in the summer. It's not *really*

15

my home. Sometimes I can't even remember what it looks like."

"It doesn't matter," he'd said. "What matters is what's in your heart. What you love."

I did love Minos, but back home, my memories of it were like a watercolor painting with the colors all smudged. Now that I was there again, I tried, with each step, to remind myself, *This is real, this is real.*

After a while of walking, Pappou and I stopped before a set of steep, downward steps. "From here, we must be careful," he said. I wanted to squeal with excitement and shout, *We're leaving the path!* But I stifled the urge; I sensed a need, alongside Pappou, for quiet.

The rocky steps were loose and broken up in some places, the cracks filled in with weeds. When I looked down at my pink and purple sneakers pressing into the dirt and kicking up pebbles, I felt like a woman of the wild, chosen by my sage and noble grandfather for an honor, of which I needed to remain worthy.

After we reached the bottom of what seemed like hundreds of steps, we came upon a valley, where a stone archway crested above a stream. "We need to cross this bridge," Pappou said. "Can you do this?"

I gazed at the stream and nodded quickly. "Yes," I said, "I can," though I wasn't sure.

"I won't be able to hold your hand," he said. "The way is too narrow."

I crept across, careful not to glance down at the water ten feet below, and he followed. By not looking down, I found it easy to pretend that this was just another part of the path, with plenty of space in the two-foot-wide bridge for my feet.

Our destination turned out to be my great uncle Stavros' home, which looked like a jungle hut, covered with greenery and fronted by a veranda that was canopied by grapevines wrapped around a pergola. "*Na toh,*" he said to my Pappou. *There it is.* He was pointing to a cardboard box at the far end of the porch. Pappou led me over to the box and told me to take a look inside. "*Kounelakia,*" he said. *Bunnies.*

I peaked inside: some large, some small, some gray, some white, some black, and others a mix, they looked to me like fat, fuzzy cats with black marbly eyes, hunched backs, and ears that weren't nearly as droopy as I would have expected rabbits' ears to be.

Pappou stepped away and sat with his brother at a small wooden table to drink Ouzo, leaving me alone with the animals. I waited for a few moments before kneeling down, leaning in, then reaching my hand toward them, slowly, ever so slowly, so as not to startle them. With my fingertips, I brushed one bunny's velvety fur as lightly as I could. The rabbit—a baby—stopped its jittering, became motionless, calmed by the touch. I leaned in, amazed by the power of my own hand. Another came close for me to pet him, too, and this time I used my palm. I softly grazed his fur, then massaged in deeper. I tried to be gentle, careful not to make a sound, trying to say, without a word, to these innocent creatures with such fear in their unblinking eyes, "I am your friend. You can trust me. I won't hurt you."

I didn't react on the outside, but inside, I felt moved and changed—wiser, for having been patient, for having controlled my desire to pick them up and squeeze them. Now, I wanted to shout, "Pappou, Pappou, they like me!" but instead I remained reserved, focused on the moment.

My whole body felt warm, the air around me a plush blanket. In the soft evening light that had just settled in, the cicadas' sharp buzz faded into the crickets' soft hum, and the whole world seemed changed: open, light, and gracious—a harboring presence, just as I felt I could be for these animals, or any other vulnerable creature who might need me ever after.

The next evening, around 4 p.m., while the rest of the family took their afternoon naps, my memory of the bunnies kept me awake. They needed me, needed to know that I hadn't forgotten them, and it was my duty to return to their side.

I made my way quietly out of the house, down the path to the steps, where I climbed down toward the valley to the same bridge I'd crossed earlier, with Pappou.

It was the perfect time of day—creamy light tempering every stone and tree, a buzz in the air like soft music. My heart felt expansive and bold, as though it had grown white feathered wings. I stepped onto the bridge and walked tepidly across. At the center, the highest point, I steadied myself, then closed my eyes and thrust my hands into the air toward the slowly retreating sun. I leaned my head back, with a smile so wide my cheeks pinched as gravity pulled them downward. I breathed in deep and let my arms fall out to my sides. My mind churned up images of all the good things—Pappou meeting us in the village as we arrived, with his donkey Calypso, who carried our luggage down the path; Calypso's teardrop eyes, like human eyes; Yiayia placing an almond cookie into my hand, the soft powdery sugar melting on my lips as I took a bite. The dusty smell of the first day of school, of pencils sharpened and heavy books cracked open for the first time in months. Our little dachshund, Herman, nestling his warm snout into the instep of my foot. The dogwood tree in our backyard. The baby blue dress my godmother bought me for Easter, with its crinoline slip, perfect for twirling; the smoothness of the satiny silk against my bare skin.

All of it seemed real, yet unreal at the same time. I felt weightless and free and connected to every living being in this world.

Until I looked down at the water below.

My footing came loose. I stumbled to the left, then right. I tried to steady myself with my arms out parallel to my shoulders, as I'd learned to do in gym class back home, but it only made things worse. My legs gave out, and my thigh scraped against the stone of the bridge before I tumbled ten feet down into the water.

Beneath the stream, I flailed and flapped my arms. The water was shallow, I knew, because I could still see the surface as I kicked at the ground, but it was too far out of reach. My body propelled forward, grasping for the open air, but it was no use.

I stopped resisting and made myself perfectly calm. I let go; I let the water take me where it would.

Choking out a cough, I finally somehow broke through the surface and paddled my way over to the shore. I dug into the soil, nails scraping at the dirt, and collapsed, my chest pressed into the muddy ground. I gagged out a hoarse cry of "Help, help, help!" though I knew there was no one around to hear me.

I fell into a deep sleep, and some time later I awoke to the sight of my Pappou above me. Not quite night yet, near dusk. "Irinie," he said, as he gripped my face. "Irinie."

Once I opened my eyes, he said no more but simply lifted me into his arms and carried me back up the steps, through the village, and to the house. My hands circled his neck, my cheek pressed into the bristly hairs of his chest, and I dozed into a twilight sleep as he held me.

Back home, my mother cried, and shrieked, "Don't you ever go off alone again," and I promised, no, I never would, as Pappou carried me through the house. He walked toward Yiayia, who approached him with intent, and he handed me off into her arms.

She cradled my head and carried me into her dark bedroom, where she laid me on a quilt and propped me up with sturdy pillows. She sat on the edge of the bed and poured drops of olive oil into a water glass, pursed three fingers together and made the sign of the cross, in a tiny gesture near my forehead, over and over, as she whispered prayers I'd never heard before, in a low and barely audible voice. In the darkness of that room she resembled a spirit, or a beam of neon light.

When the prayers were done, she held me tightly in her arms, then lifted the glass into the air. "See?" she said. "The drops of oil have grown larger. Someone—who knows who, my precious baby—has given you the *mati*. But you are better now. Don't worry. You are strong, and you are blessed."

Yet I didn't feel blessed.

That night, I had a nightmare. Considering its elements alone, it shouldn't have been frightening—a placid, slow-moving river in the woods, a clear blue sky above, weeping cherry trees draping their branches down listlessly like fingertips grazing the water's surface, the entire scene swept in a pale blue, green, yellow, and crimson palette; the sweet scent of jasmine emanating from the banks. And me, sitting in an oblong canoe, with a sleepy-eyed man wearing a floppy, beige sun hat who stood on the edge of the boat, paddling slowly, a thin smile spread across his wrinkled face.

Still, something about that dream was terrifying. The sinister delicacy of the paddling, the mocking lightness of the oar grazing the water, the rippling so contained; the subtle splash of wood penetrating water and then being swallowed whole, with barely a sound or sight, until its helpless reemergence. In the stillness, the tranquil scene, a horror lurked; a sense that a whole, consuming world existed below the surface, but I couldn't see it. I couldn't do anything, in fact; I couldn't move, think, or even speak.

Then I dreamt of a fiery train crash, two engines burst apart in a head-on collision. But I was not seeing it directly, only knew of it through the omniscience of dreaming. Instead, I remained on that boat, alone and remote, being guided to a place serene yet far from peace, with no ability to resist or intervene, while disaster occurred elsewhere.

CHAPTER THREE
THE NIGHT BEFORE

It was around 8 p.m. last night when I decided to venture out. The night before, I'd barely slept, despite the hour I spent racing on the elliptical machine under the bright industrial Rec Plex lights, and the several I spent reading in bed. When I did fall asleep, it felt like an actual fall—a rough and clunky tumble into a series of nightmares: of airplanes crashing into towers, a massive plume of black smoke enveloping the city streets and buildings, shops, and sidewalks full of people. I awoke in the thickness of the dark, my fists clenched, my jaw tight, my heart racing, and with sweat pasting the nape of my neck.

Zombied, I reached my arm up to the desk beside my sagging twin bed and grabbed the wooden icon my Yiayia had sent me for my birthday a few months ago, from the holy island of Tinos. I made the sign of the cross three times and kissed the image of the Virgin Mary holding baby Jesus. "I'm sorry," I whispered, to no one—because it seemed to me that the dream itself could only have been spawned by some negative thought or idea my own mind had sheltered; and that dream, in turn, could cause God-only-knows what other harm if not atoned.

Next, I reached for the glass owl eye—the blue *mati* bead— she'd also sent me in the same air-mailed care package. The eye is supposed to protect you from curses, from evil spirits and energies, from all the unseen negative forces you are vulnerable to, or unwittingly invite. I wasn't sure which—or if either—of these objects could actually protect me, but I gripped them both just in case.

So yesterday, after going through all that the night before, I opted for a different approach: to go out, and truly tire myself out, in hopes of slipping into a more natural, peaceful, and deeper type of slumber.

Not that I had anyone to go out with, or anywhere in particular to go. I've always been a bit of a lone wolf, but that's been especially the case here at college. Despite being a junior, it's my first year living on campus. The last two years, I lived in an apartment with my sister Eugenia, who went to school across the city. Eugenia and I were together all the time. Most nights, all we did was drive around in her midnight-blue Toyota Corolla with the stereo blasting. Genie drove, while I managed the radio and air temperature.

My sophomore year, most weekends, I traveled home to visit my boyfriend, Steve, or he came up to visit me. I'd met Steve at a party back home during the summer after freshman year, and he became my boyfriend—my first, really, because I've never been the boyfriend type; I've always been more of the *friend* type, the type guys came to for help with their girlfriends.

But Steve and I aren't together anymore, and Eugenia graduated, moved home to Rhode Island in search of a job, so it made sense to move on campus. To try to live the normal college life.

And I felt glad to do so, really. I knew the place only by day: in the fresh morning air, the sunlight shining above the belltower, with packs of fresh-faced students lounging in the courtyards or bustling down the clean sidewalks cutting through the perfectly-manicured, shiny-green lawns.

I even looked forward to the dorm, to having a confined

space all my own—even if it was only half of an already small room. The size of my half entitled me to it fully. In preparation, I collected a stack of magazines, flyers, and newspapers from around my parents' home and combed through each page, clipping images, phrases, and words—like, "Be your own," which I paired with another scrap that simply said "mind," and I posted it above a picture of a field of pink and purple wildflowers.

On move-in day, I spent three hours taping these bits of paper around my bed and desk, careful not to hang them up too high on the walls, so as not to impose on my roommate, Kathryn.

Kathryn and I were randomly paired by the school. From what I can tell, she had a sort of falling out with her friends and resigned herself to the powers of the university housing office. I had done the same because I had no friends at this school, and because I had faith that it would all work out—she and I would turn instant friends, eating dinner together and watching mindless television after a long day of classes and library time. We'd hang out with the other girls on our floor every weekend. While getting dressed, we'd sip fruity wine and dance to pop music, and we'd style each other's hair and apply each other's makeup (I'd start wearing it) and tell each other how great we looked, plotting the fun we'd have and strategies for the night. Afterward, we'd gather on the couch to gossip and pore over every detail, who said what to whom.

But things haven't exactly started out that way. Kathryn managed to bandage her friendships over the summer and is working on regaining half the friends she "won in the divorce" from the one girl with whom, she says, she is entirely done forever. And all the other girls on our floor have their own, separate network of friends built up over the last three years, and they see no advantage in befriending a junior with no alliances of her own, a near untouchable in the campus caste system.

Between my usual issues with sleep and the fact of Grandma's death, I've been feeling kind of . . . off. So I needed a distraction last night. A simple evening out on the town by myself. My plan was to meander down Newbury Street as a groupless observer of the reveling crowds. I decided it was time to forget all that stuff about being a normal college kid and start accepting who I am. I dressed and packed a notebook, pen, and book into my green canvas tote bag, ready to be unknown and unseen among the masses. But stepping out into the hallway, I bumped abruptly into one of the girls from down the hall, named Agnes Magyar.

I met Agnes during a hall meeting on move in night, when our R.A. paired us up during a "getting-to-know-you" type deal. A girl named Daniella, whom I'd known from a psychology class last year, and who had observed my awkward conversation with Agnes, approached me after the meeting and warned me that Agnes was not a girl to mess with, a real drama queen. I cast that off as inconsequential, since I'd never "messed with" anyone in my life. And plus, I tended not to trust other people's perceptions of other people.

But Agnes, indeed, was a staggering presence—tall, with broad, athletic shoulders and a deep, resounding voice. She had an icy look, with hard blue eyes and white-blonde hair. Just short of colliding with her last night in the hallway, I gasped and stumbled backward. "Sorry," I said.

Agnes looked at me for what seemed like the first time ever and said, "Where are *you* going?"

How does she know I'm going somewhere? I wondered, until I glanced down at my fitted yellow V-neck, my crisp new jeans, the braided leather belt I bought three years ago but never wore. Not the usual pajama pants and oversized T-shirt she'd probably seen me wearing around the halls and common areas. "Just heading downtown," I said, a sheepish smile betraying my uneasiness. "Getting a little stir crazy in this dorm, ya know?" The word "crazy" came out feeling a little too much like itself.

Agnes curled her lip. "By yourself?"

I shrugged and smiled shyly. "Yeah. I don't mind it. I—"

She squinted her eyes. "Why don't you come out with us?"

The pleasantness of the invitation surprised me, and I saw no clear way to refuse. "Um . . . yeah, sure. Thanks. If you don't mind. I mean, I . . ."

"Come down to our room when you're ready," she said, focused on her cell phone now. She looked at me from head to toe. "The other girls are there, too," she added, confident in my knowing who "the other girls" were. And I did—I'd seen her with her clique of friends together in the cafeteria and all over the dorm building, and one of them once asked if I'd seen Agnes. I hadn't, but I have to admit, it had felt good to be asked.

Agnes's dorm apartment resembled ours—a combo living room and kitchen with a shared bedroom—but with different tapestries, cheaply-framed Dali prints, and Bob Marley posters. It smelled like a mix of floral shampoo and whiskey. Inside, four girls scrambled about, prepping for the evening. Agnes barked out introductions, which resulted in a series of "heys," and "yos," and smiles and waves. A short blonde girl named Sylvie popped her head out from the bathroom, a curling iron hoisted by her ear, and smiled at me, then squeaked to the others, "Are the guys waiting for us outside?"

"Let them wait," a sharp voice cut in. It was Brittany, Agnes's roommate. She wore a purple, scoop-neck tee shirt, tight in the chest and waist, with ripped jeans and a nose ring. She stood in front of the mirror by the door, fluffed her curly brown hair, checked her teeth, and when she said, "Okay, ladies. Let's go," the whole group assembled.

I was in awe.

We marched in a pack toward the elevators—five girls on a mission, a posse; tough chicks ready for a night out partying. *Why am I wearing yellow?* I thought for a fleeting moment, but I brushed the thought aside and assumed the pose.

We found the two guys who had apparently been waiting for us perched on a brick wall behind the building. One, with a wide, open grin and a boyish haircut, sidled up to Brittany, who shot him a stony glare. "Where are you going in those pink pants?" she snapped.

He looked down in surprise. "What's the matter with my pink pants?"

"They're *pink pants*." She turned to me then with a thin smile and said, "Rinie, this is Charlie. Charlie, Rinie." I waved, and he offered a simple "What's up?"

Meanwhile, the other guy—shaggy brown hair, torn faded jeans, distracted brown eyes—remained seated on the wall, puffing a cigarette. Brittany pointed her chin in his direction and said, "That's Andy." I waved at him, too, and said hi, and he responded with a quick nod, a deep inhale, and a "How's it goin'" on the exhale. *This guy is either really cool, or really thinks he is,* I thought.

"All right, everybody in the car," Agnes called. She stood fumbling with her keys beside a sleek white Lexus SUV parked in the fire lane. "*Now!*"

"Chill out, Agnes," said Sylvie.

"Don't tell me to chill out, girl. I'm the one driving your asses."

The squeaky-voiced girl rolled her eyes. "Please, like you'd have it any other way."

"There's no way we're all fitting in here," Charlie said, with a hand on the roof and his head ducked in.

"We fit," Agnes snapped.

"No *way* we fit."

Agnes glared at him. "All right, then, you take the T."

"Not *me*. I'm riding with Britt."

All through this, my cheeks warmed like a hotplate. My skin burned beneath the street lamp. Part of me wanted to shout, "Me! I'll take the T!" And then sneak off somewhere else entirely.

But I didn't, because doing so would have diverted all those eyes to me, and then I'd have to ward off all those "don't be sillies," since I was the newcomer, the only one to whom they still needed to be polite. I could see no way to say, "Really, I don't mind. I *want* to take the T," and be honestly believed.

"*I'll* take the T," a girl named Katie, the quietest of the group, said. "C'mon, Sylvie. Come with me." So the two girls departed for the train, while the rest of us—Agnes, Brittany, Charlie, Andy, and I—took our places in the car.

"You sit front," Agnes said to me. With no sense of a choice, I obliged.

As the car pulled out of the school parking lot, Charlie shouted, "Yo, Andy, you gonna share?"

I turned my head to see Andy lifting a silver flask into the air. Britt, who sat between the two guys, grabbed it and took a swig, then gestured it toward me.

"Hey, hey, what about me?" Charlie whined.

"You'll get yours," Brittany said, looking not at him but at me. "The new girl's gotta go first."

Charlie leaned forward, squishing the right of his thigh into Brittany's knees, and tapped my shoulder. "Hey, what's your name again? *Reensie?*"

"Rinie," I said, taking hold of the object and trying to steady my voice. "Short for Irinie."

"What kinda name is that? Why not just *Irene?*"

I gazed at the flask in my hand for a moment as if it held the answer. "It's Greek," I said. And then—in thoughtless habit—I added, "It means *peace*."

"Hey, now!" Charlie shouted, so abrasively my body lurched backward. "Peace, huh?" He rubbed his chin with a thumb and forefinger. "So. Do you live up to your name?"

I sipped hard and let the liquid burn my throat. "I try to," I gasped in a voice raspier than I expected, and everyone in the car laughed.

"Leave the girl alone," Brittany chimed in, jabbing Charlie in the arm.

"What did I do?" He raised his bent arms. "I'm trying to be friendly."

Brittany pursed her lips and narrowed her eyes. "Well, don't." She turned to face front and held her hand out for the flask.

We arrived at the bar, about a mile or two from campus, and remained there for about an hour, downing cocktails, beers, and shots, and singing along to the cover songs played by the band—the usual tunes like Kenny Rogers' "The Gambler," The Rolling Stones' "Sympathy for the Devil," Lynyrd Skynyrd's "Freebird." In that time, I drank two glasses of house white wine and took a Lemon Drop shooter.

I haven't been much of a drinker in the last few years. Not since I was a junior in high school, when I prided myself on being the only girl who could gulp straight from a bottle of warm Vodka and not throw up or black out. My friends chalked it up to the Greek in me, since it didn't fit with the rest of how they saw me—the shy, more seemingly timid and harmless parts. But this ability to take down harsh liquor with ease had nothing to do with my Greekness. It had to do with either a complete naivety, or else a keen awareness of how inconsequential that sting really was, how fleeting and unlike real pain. Whatever it was that gave me this rogue skill, it made me feel strong and undeterrable.

But by the following year, I stopped drinking all together, for two important reasons: one, I became too conscious of how drinking eroded my sense of control, and control had become increasingly important to me; two, alcohol contained too many calories, and I'd developed the habit, or compulsion, of severely restricting such things.

Last night, though, felt different. Or like the *start* of something different. Camaraderie. Communion with others. The way they called me "the new girl" made me feel that I would inevitably become the reverse some day, one of the crowd, and that meant something. It meant, for one, no more lonely Friday nights with melodramatic music and my journal. It meant distraction. The distraction I needed, if only to be able to sleep.

When we left the first bar for another one down the block, I let the evening air overtake me, and as I did, my body began to feel weightless, propped up and propelled by a surge of life coursing through it. We walked in a scattered pack and I drifted off to the side so I could revel in these moments of silence. Really take them in. I looked up toward the sky, to the stars just dimly peeking out, and thought, *Life really is good.*

"Rinie," Agnes called out. "Come over here and settle this for us." I skipped over to where she stood with Brittany. They laughed, though I wasn't sure why.

"Brittany says I can be a real bitch to people I don't know. Is that true? Am I a bitch to people I don't know?"

I thought about the moment I met Agnes, in the dorm building elevator. "Who are *you?*" was the first thing she said, with no smile, no eye contact.

"No, you're not a bitch," I said. "You're just . . . reserved. And . . . direct."

"*Thank* you," Agnes said, with a smirk.

"She's just being *nice*," Brittany said to Agnes, and then to me: "You don't have to be so *nice*, Rinie."

The final destination for the evening was aptly named *The Dive*. Most of us circled around a sticky table in the back corner, while Andy went straight for the bar. He returned moments later with a tray full of tequila shots.

"Good man!" Charlie yelped, slapping his back.

Andy held up his drink and shouted, "Prost! Everybody, *prost!*"

The group obliged, echoing, "Prost!" and took a collective swig.

Agnes wiped her mouth and demanded, "What's that, 'prost'?"

Andy banged his glass down on the table, leaned forward, and said, "It's *German*." He leaned back and wagged a finger through the air as he spoke. "You know? Europe is a categorically superior continent. I spent the past summer traveling around Germany, which is by far the best country in Europe. Which means," he paused, "it is the best country in the world."

This incited a clamor of protests and offered alternatives—Italy, France, The Netherlands. "And what about Asia?" someone said. "The oldest civilizations in the world!"

But I knew to stay out of this one. Growing up surrounded by Greek men always trying to out-drink, out-earn, out-spend, and out-argue one another taught me a thing or two about male bravado. People saying these things only *sometimes* believed them, but in most cases, they were simply seeking reactions from others. The best way to discourage such behavior was to not engage with it.

As the conversation splintered off again, Andy scooted his chair closer to mine, which affirmed my new view of him as an insecure man seeking approval, and a reaction, from *everyone*. "So," he said, nudging me in the elbow. "You're a Greek girl."

I was taken aback, at first, by his knowing this, until I remembered it came up in the car, with the name thing. "I am," I said slowly.

"Greece, huh?" He rubbed his chin in mock thoughtfulness. "Nobody goes to Greece." He smacked his hand on the table again, setting the shot glasses dancing.

I smiled and paused, careful not to take the bait. "I don't think that's actually true," I said, "but okay."

"Eh, nobody goes there." He waved the idea away and grinned.

"Okay, nobody goes there." I laughed and shrugged.

"Greece is for suckers." He smiled a squinty-eyed smile.

I laughed again—it's what I do, when I don't know what else to do—and shook my head. "Whatever you say."

My nonengagement tactics seemed to be working because he changed the course of conversation. "Where are you from?" he asked, still grinning. "*Other* than Greece."

I appreciated the humor; with my olive skin and dark, curly hair, people often ask me that question, especially in the summer, with my skin freshly tanned. I know what kind of answer they're seeking—something exotic—which is why I find it funny to say "Rhode Island." "Rhode Island," I said to Andy. "It's just my father who is from Greece."

"And what does your dad do, run a diner?" He jabbed me in the arm playfully.

"Actually, yeah he does."

Andy, I learned, was from New Jersey—right outside New

York City. "Lots of diners down there," he said.

"I love Manhattan," I said. "I love a good city."

Yes, Andy agreed with his squinty-eyed smile. A good city is essential. So we talked about cities—about the life of them, their culture, their vibe, and how each of us couldn't imagine going to college in a place without a city at least nearby. "You get so sick of these college parties after a while," he said, leaning forward. "The same people. The same dull, meaningless conversations." I nodded, even though I hadn't actually attended many of these parties myself, because I knew about that meaninglessness.

"How come I haven't seen you around before?" he asked. It seemed an odd question. Why would he have seen me around? But I guess it's a smaller world here than I know. So I explained my situation—my sister, the ex-boyfriend, the living off campus. "You're lucky," he said. "You're uncorrupted."

I remember laughing and rolling my eyes. It seemed so absurd a statement at the time. In fact, *corrupted* is exactly how I've been feeling lately—and for the last few years. As if something in me has been decaying—at times slowly, at times more rapidly—and, try as I might, there is no reversing the damage. Hearing him say "You're uncorrupted" made me feel it, that sense of decay, in a way I could identify and name. And the recognition, at least for a moment, seemed to help. It felt good.

No one took the train home that night. Emboldened by my drunkenness, I insisted on being the one to climb into the way back of Agnes's SUV. I offered the excuse that I'd accepted the front seat on the way down, and it was only fair, but in reality, I wanted a break from all the commotion.

On the drive toward campus, I lay on my back, my head at

rest on the hump of the tire, and I focused my eyes and all my conscious energy on one point in the ceiling. I allowed my body to roll at will from side to side without resisting. A Kanye West song blared from the speakers.

This, I thought, is exactly what I need: to be near the liveliness of others, but at a safe distance; and, preferably, in an altered state of mind; one that could free me from the incessant pressing of thoughts. The drinks left me buoyant—my body rocked back and forth as if floating in a stream of air I normally had no access to.

While I stared into the roof, assessing the symmetry of the air conditioning vents, Andy's face invaded my view as he perched above the back seat. He smiled—that squinty-eyed smile again—and he winked. *He gets it,* I thought. *He knows this feeling, too.*

The car came to a halt in the lot near the dorm building, and as I climbed over the seat, I overheard Charlie inviting Agnes and Brittany back to his and Andy's place, "to smoke some bud." Andy winked at me again—ever so slightly, barely discernibly—as Charlie added, "Bring the new girl, too." They stood beside the car, under the bright streetlamp of the mostly empty parking lot. Sylvie and Katie had disappeared into the darkness.

"I think we can do that," Agnes said. She turned to Brittany, and then to me. "What do you think, ladies?"

"I guess we can do that," Brittany shrugged.

"Sure," I said, my voice chipper and high. I had smoked weed a couple of times in high school—after the prom, graduation. I could handle this. *This is college,* I thought. *Late night partying. People to stay awake with.*

So we made the trek across campus, past the sounds of drunken laughter, waves of music floating through open windows, clusters of students prowling through the alleys between buildings, before we made it up to Charlie and Andy's dorm, where we assembled on a black L-shaped leather couch in their common room. Charlie turned the television on but muted it, with the stereo blasting over, which made everything on the screen seem overdramatized—entrancingly absurd. *I like these people,* I thought.

With every inhale of the joint that was passed, I felt closer and closer to each person. The room filled with the sweet scent of smoke, which made it feel dreamlike. "You feel me, man?" I heard Charlie say—not just to the other man in the room, but to all of us.

"Word," someone said in return. Brittany, maybe. It didn't matter who anymore—but I laughed at what was said and nodded my head, happy with the concept: word is affirmative, word is truth.

Andy, seated beside me, said in a low voice, "What's funny?"

I laughed again and said, "Nothing. I just laugh sometimes . . ."

"I like that." He leaned into my side, and as I felt the warmth of his arm on mine, my own bare toes suddenly felt too cold, so I slid them beneath his thigh.

He glanced at me and smiled. "You're one of them," he said. "Cold toes. I can feel them through my jeans."

I looked down at my lap and smiled shyly, feeling naked. I thought to remove my toes, but they felt so warm, and it had been so long since my toes had been warm beneath somebody else's thighs. So I stared straight at the television screen. A re-run of *Seinfeld.* Characters shouting, laughing, waving their arms, shaking cereal boxes, silently and frantically wreaking havoc as the R. Kelly song "Ignition" crooned through the speakers. So what, he's drunk . . .

"Later, you two." The sound of Agnes's voice, calling from

where she stood by the door, awoke me to the fact that I'd entered a strange sort of warp zone, alone in it with Andy. Brittany and Charlie were no longer in the room. How much time had gone by? I had no idea.

"Later," Andy grunted, not moving; not even looking up. Agnes closed the door behind her.

I sat up a bit then. But didn't remove my toes. "Wait, where is she going?" I asked. "I should go after her . . ." I moved even farther forward but still did not remove those toes.

Andy kept his eyes on the television. "She's fine," he said. "Trust me." Then he turned to me, put a warm hand on my thigh and let it rest, and I sat back into the couch cushion. He pushed his body again against my side, then leaned in, cupped his other hand to my face, and pressed his mouth to mine. I kissed him back and let my whole body sink down off of me, as if all my weight and mass had melted like ice and drained away. "Let's go to my room," Andy said after a minute or two. "For more privacy."

My body tensed. "Let's stay here," I said. "I don't want to move . . ." I closed my eyes and leaned back, to emphasize my own tiredness, and as I did, I felt a real, authentic sleepiness— the kind I normally craved; in fact, doggedly pursued. "I could just fall asleep right now . . ." I said, rolling my head in a circle.

"C'mon," he said. "Not here. I have a nice, warm bed in there."

He stood and grabbed hold of my hand to help me up. *I can do this,* I thought, as I let him pull me upright. *I can just fall right to sleep.* He led me down the hall and into his room.

There was a photograph on his desk in a simple black frame—the first thing I saw as I entered—of a woman with sunny blonde hair and one of the widest, most engulfing smiles I've ever seen; white, imperfect teeth, happy with themselves, out in the air celebrating, a head thrown back in abandon, with

36

a cartoonishly blue sky and white clouds as a backdrop.

"Who is that?" I said, pointing, without a second thought, to the image.

"My mom," he said stiffly, and I saw him then as a five-year-old boy, this ebullient woman brushing his dusty brown hair with a delicate hand; a knowing smile in my direction, saying, "Don't mind my boy, he's shy."

"She's beautiful," I said.

He couldn't hold back a grin as his eyes cast over the picture. "She's the most amazing woman in the world. There is no one like her." He looked away, then, from the photo and said, "That one's mine," pointing to the twin bed on the right. "I gotta take a leak."

I dove onto the bed as he left the room and curled my knees into my chest, facing the wall. *Sleep,* I thought. *Just sleep. By the time he gets back, you'll be out.*

A minute or two later, he returned to the room. Through the slightest slits of my eyes, I could see him walk over to his computer. "What's your screen name?" he asked.

I said nothing until he asked again, and then I grumbled, "Rinie11."

He typed on the computer long enough, I thought, to make it believable that I could be sleeping when he joined me in bed.

Still facing the wall, I shifted my weight deeper into the sheets, with my arm now shielding my face. *Just keep pretending to sleep,* I thought. He reached for my thigh and tried to turn my body toward him. "C'mon," he whispered. "Just give me a kiss. All I want is a kiss." He rocked my hip a few times gently. "C'mon."

One kiss, and he'll let me sleep, I thought. So I let him turn my body halfway and I kissed him, lazily, and let it end fast. He rubbed my legs, my stomach, my chest. As I leaned again toward the wall, his hands, the rubbing, kept pressing me toward him.

In a way, it felt good to have this man's warm hands on my body. It felt good to be so relaxed, and a little bit out of my mind from the weed and the drinks. It felt good to hear this handsome man saying, "Trust me."

But now I sensed the consequences. The payment for that comfort and warmth, that abandon. The pinch of my own foolishness pricked my mind out of that tranquilizing fog.

I opened my eyes, sat up and said, staring him straight in the eyes, "Listen. We can't have sex."

He sat up a bit, now, too. "Why not?"

Why not? How could I explain why not? How could I explain that, before Steve, I'd barely ever kissed any boys? That I grew up in a nice, church-going family and wasn't supposed to do these types of things, be in these places. That I chose, in my life, not to believe in regret and didn't know how I would avoid letting this become one; that this wasn't me, that I was only in this bed because I was reeling, desperate for human connection, quietly out of control, and that I needed someone to save me right now, from myself—needed to believe and trust that someone could; that someone could see and respect the overriding hurt and fear and confusion that led to this need for anesthetization tonight. That I needed it, and needed it to be enough.

"We just can't," I said. "I'm sorry. I really am sorry."

He leaned in and kissed me again, and I felt the relief of being understood, of having somehow spoken my silent thoughts and having them *heard*.

But moments later, his fingers crept down my stomach to the button of my jeans. I, gently, tried to brush them away. A reminder.

He moved them back.

I tried to push and then pry the hand away, but his grip

held tighter than mine, tighter this time. He unbuttoned my pants in one swift move, unzipped, slipped both hands down my back, then swept them down my hips. He slipped his thumbs into my belt loops and yanked down the jeans. As he did, I pushed my forearms against his, to create an opposing force, but he pulled harder.

"No," I whispered. "I'm cold."

He said nothing. I felt invisible; more than invisible, like I'd disappeared completely. He hovered above me and pulled the jeans over my ankles, along with my underwear, and tossed them to the floor.

"No," I whispered again.

With one hand, he pulled off his underwear, while the other hand slid onto the small of my back. I placed my thumbs along his pelvis, my hands wrapped just halfway around his hips. As he leaned his body onto mine, grabbed my waist, and bore down, I tried to push him up, off, *out.*

But it was too late. Too little.

It wasn't long before he was done with me. He collapsed onto me, his arms splayed out to the side, his chest pressed hard against mine. A tear rolled down my cheek, and I felt a finger, his finger, reach up to catch it.

Then I curled in toward the wall, and took the sleep I'd earned.

Chapter Four
Age Eight

"You can do it," Mark said. "Just let go."

I stood on his lap, a slippery eight-year-old in a mermaid bathing suit. He held me with his muscle-toned arms by the armpits—my big brother.

"*No!*" I wailed, my butt bearing down on his chest. "I *can't!*"

"Rinie, you gotta stop being so afraid all the time," he said. At seventeen, he had the firm, commanding voice of a man. "Just do it!"

He'd brought me to the beach that day with his friends, and I'd spent most of my time digging in the sand as they conducted their chicken fights and played volleyball in their swim trunks and bikinis. But at a certain point, Mark drifted from the crowd long enough to notice I hadn't entered the water all day. "I'm fine here," I'd said. "I'm working on a sea turtle."

He towered over me, shaking his head. "Not a very good sea turtle. Come on, let's go."

As he led me into the cold water, I wrapped my arm tightly around his. We swam for a bit, and I gradually grew more comfortable floating and bopping around. But I wouldn't venture underwater. Now, Mark held me by the arms, facing away from him, and demanded that I leap from his knees. I knew it wouldn't be a simple jump, that he would toss me into the air with enough force that I would sink beneath the surface, so I wasn't having it.

"No!" I shouted. "I *hate* you!"

"I don't care," he said, his eyebrows arched in a way that told me he meant it. "Do it," he said, "or I'll never talk to you again."

Though I knew this wasn't likely, it was also not a risk I was willing to take. Mark's affection for me was crucial. He was the perfect brother. The perfect everything—student council president, captain of the soccer team, on his way to college scholarships and the homecoming court. One of those people who sweep through life like it's a perfectly choreographed dance, or a play in which he is cast as the humble lead. He played Barbies with me—always agreed to be my Ken doll, but refused to let Ken be my Barbie's boyfriend. "You're too young to be thinking about boyfriends," he said, gently tugging at both of my earlobes. "Ken is just a *friend*."

He held my hand on the way in to church every Sunday and told me I looked pretty in my dress; he'd ask me to spin around so he could get a better look and would say, each time, "Gorgeous!" He had a beautiful girlfriend named Crystal who always said "Hi, Rinie!" when I answered the phone, before asking, "Is your brother around?" The two of them took me for ice cream downtown not long after Mark got his license. He let me hang out in his bedroom sometimes, even when his friends were over, and I would color at his desk while they listened to music and played poker with pennies, until my time was up. "Okay, squirt. That's enough for today. Go on up to your own room now." And I would leave with no complaint, because I knew I was lucky to be there in the first place, in his orbit of kindness and charm.

Yet he was hard on me, too: he expected me to be strong, not a scared little girl.

There was no way out of this situation other than through the jump. He wasn't going to give it up. So I sucked in my breath, shut my eyes, pinched my nose, and screeched like a baby pterodactyl as I leapt into the water. I flew pretty high into the air but quickly discovered that the water was shallow enough that my feet hit the sand within seconds, and I bounced from the bottom, my nose still plugged, my chin barely penetrating the surface.

"See?" he shouted as I spun around to face him. "I knew you could do it!"

I laughed.

"It wasn't really all that difficult, was it? Doesn't matter. I'm proud of you." He pulled me up from the water into his arms and swung me in a circle, my legs fanning out like the ribbon on a maypole. When he set me back to earth, I jumped up and down, shouting, "Again! Again!"

He did it, again and again, and I got braver and braver an inch at a time.

"We're going in deeper, now," he declared after several rounds. "This is getting too easy."

"No," I said. "That's enough."

But it wasn't. Mark led me in to where my feet couldn't touch the ground, and then let me go. I panicked at the feeling of that weightlessness as I kicked at nothing, and sunk beneath the water. I flailed my arms and swallowed a sharp, salty mouthful before managing to swim the ten feet back into his arms.

I coughed out the water and cried like a baby, I pounded his suntanned chest and yelled, "I hate you! I hate you! I hate you! I will never trust you again!"

He hugged me tight, and immediately, I felt safe; I forgave Mark the moment he did so. But I didn't tell him that. I didn't say anything—I didn't talk to him the whole ride home from the beach—even when he played my favorite songs in the car or as he tapped out the sand from my sneakers in our driveway.

I didn't talk to him that evening during dinner; didn't say a word as he came into my bedroom to say goodbye before he went back out for the night with his friends. I refused to look up from my book as he walked over to the bed and brushed my hair behind my ear.

"You'll forgive me some day, squirt," he said, and then walked out the door.

A couple hours later, I was in my bedroom, half-reading a chapter book and half-listening to the Top Twenty countdown on the radio, when the telephone rang. I ran in to Genie's room to pick it up. Genie was at a friend's house. Even though the ringing had stopped long enough for me to know that someone else had answered the call, I picked it up anyway; I was nosy like that. "Mrs. Pothos," I heard a man's voice say, "there's been an accident."

I heard the "Oh!" in both ears, the one pressed against the plastic phone receiver and the open one that was able to hear my mother downstairs in the kitchen. It sounded as though she had fallen from a chair; a sound of both surprise and pain. I immediately hung up the phone, as gently as I could, as if I hadn't heard a thing; as if that might make it stop happening, whatever it was. The connection wasn't as immediate for me— *an accident.* My brother, out driving with his friends.

I didn't survive the funeral; I felt dead throughout the whole thing. But I held onto Vicky's hand and, at one point, I dug into her palm so hard it bled.

She didn't say a word at the time, and afterward, she said she hadn't even noticed. She'd been crying too hard. Everyone cried—Genie, Vicky, Grandma, Thio Niko, my parents, Mark's friends, even my father, who—as far as I could tell—had never cried before in his life. He sobbed, for a minute, like a baby. Crystal gave a speech, too. With her silky auburn hair, perfectly neat, wearing her perfectly pressed black sweater and skirt, she read from a page of loose-leaf paper that rattled as she held it in her shaking hands. She talked about how kind Mark was, to everyone in their school, and especially to her; how he had dropped her off safely a mere fifteen minutes before the reckless drunk driver forced him off the road; how she knew he would have forgiven the driver, because that was how he lived. How all the teachers loved him, and all the awards he won were more than well-deserved. How he loved his family more than anything else in this world.

She said all of this between cries. Everyone cried but me. As the cantors hummed, as the smoky scent of incense filled the air, as the priest sang, "Holy God, Holy Mighty, Holy Immortal, Have Mercy on Us," again and again, I stared blankly at the wood of Mark's casket, a gleaming, shiny oak, polished and draped with flowers and baby's breath. I stared, immobile, a stone.

My mother cried so hard she was laughing. Tears shot from her eyes like they do in cartoons. She was hysterical in every sense of the term. They'd given her pills—"they" being all the ladies from church who came over to take care of her, to tend to all the things she needed to still see done: the mopping, the cooking, the running of the dishwasher. "Just sit, honey, sit," Thia Sophia kept telling her. I wished they would let her do something: scrub a pan, rinse a dish, peel a carrot—anything to make her feel normal. Anything to make her *look* normal, to me. Instead she appeared more like an animal, held down, fighting to get at the sink. "Just sit," they kept telling her as she wailed.

The pills were called Lorazepam, which I later learned were

tranquilizers, and which I also thought of as something given to rabid animals. I found out what the pills were because I snuck into her bathroom in the middle of the night after the wake and read the bottle, then looked it up on the Internet. I had to turn the volume off on the computer so they couldn't hear the loud swish and bonk of the dialing modem.

During the funeral, my father gripped my mother by her biceps during the parts of the service where the priest asked everyone to stand, and then he slowly let her go, let her crumple back down to the pew, when it was time to sit.

There was *that* for him to do, and that's how he survived. Vicky had Genie to take care of, and Genie had me. I, for my part, wanted to have them all—but I was trapped inside myself, imagining what it was like to be Mark—separated from everyone by a dark, dense cloud of obscurity. Removed, gone. I was dead.

It was easy to stay dead for a few days. Visitors trailed through the house, a welcome distraction. The men drank whiskey in the basement with my father, while the women maintained their occupation of our kitchen. Genie and Vicky locked themselves in their bedrooms and talked on the phone with their friends, listened to music, painted their nails, or whatever else they were doing to get by. I sat with my knees pulled up to my chest on the couch in the living room, within sight of the women, letting them pat my head or cheek as they ambled by.

It was in the days after all that, when I came back to life, that reality set in.

It started in my gut. It felt like someone had vacuum-sucked my organs out, leaving a fleshy ribcage aching for what it had lost. When I returned to school after one week off, all I could do was wrap my arms around my waist and push hard on my belly, to keep my insides in. Every hour, I had to be excused to the restroom, because I thought I might puke. I locked myself in a stall and faced the toilet, hovered above it and gagged, but nothing came out. Not once.

Everyone was so nice to me, which made everything worse. It made me remember the acrid, saccharine smell of all those carnations and lilies at the wake. Sickeningly sweet.

After that, the feeling moved on to my heart. Life, and the world, seemed breakable, sad; everywhere, I saw sadness—in the helpless chubby fingers of the man counting change for my father at the gas station; in the diner customer sitting alone in a booth, desperately devouring his meatloaf sandwich, eyes darting around, as if a predator might stalk over at any moment and steal it away; in old Mrs. Hannifan walking her small white puppy down our street: the creature dumb and blissful, the woman slow and panting.

Mark's cologne by the bathroom sink; the towel he used the night he died, hanging on the door for more than a week, growing drier and drier each day.

Lastly, it spread to my mind.

It began with guilt. Why Mark? Why him? Why not me? Why had I been the lucky one, blessed by my Yiayia all those years ago, freed from the threat of the *mati?* He took care of me. Made me brave. And what did I do? I told him I *hated* him. He died thinking I hadn't forgiven him. I'd been selfish, concerned with my own safety all the time. Never thinking for a minute that Mark, or anyone else, could die. If I'd thought of it, maybe I could have done something. Protected him. Warded it off. Instead, I courted it.

Then came fear. What would come next? When would calamity strike again?

Riding the unseatbelted bus home became a tormenting

hour of each school day, as I sat alone in total silence, clutching the torn brown leather bench-seat beneath me. I sat close to the front, alert to every snow bank, stop sign, and car on the road. I never stood and yelled to the bus driver, "Watch out!"—but it helped to know that I could.

The kids I used to sit with, joke and laugh with—the same kids who were so nice to me in the days after Mark died—seemed within a couple weeks to have forgotten entirely that my brother was *never coming back*. They asked at first why I was so quiet, why I didn't sit with them in the back rows anymore, why I never seemed to move at all, why I was so frozen in place and barely breathing, but I pretended not to know what they were talking about and said, "I'm fine." It was embarrassing, but it didn't matter. I had no choice. My sanity was at stake.

At night in bed, I kept vigil over the house, remained perfectly still to hear every sound—any motion of the man who, I was sure, lived in the furnace room, just waiting for the perfect moment to strike. My plan was to take the giraffe lamp on my desk and wait behind the door, then swing it as he passed down the hallway. I'd creep out to the kitchen and call the police, then hide under the table.

Or I would duck under the covers and pretend it wasn't happening.

I listened for the wind, to note if it blew too hard, which might signal a tornado or a terrible storm that could fell a tree onto our house. I sniffed the air for the scent of smoke in case of fire, or what I imagined to be the smell of natural gas or carbon monoxide. I'd seen the commercials. These were deadly.

One night, my mother was cleaning the oven, and the rancid smell of food scraps burning off at 600 degrees drove me to panic. Even though I normally tried not to reveal the sources of danger to anyone else, in a superstitious belief that doing so might make them all the more real, and even though it meant the risk of running square into the furnace-room killer, I leaped out of bed and ran through the house, into my parents' bedroom. "What is that smell?" I shouted. "Wake up, wake up! What is that smell?"

They explained it was the stove, the cleaning.

"No, no, it smells like something else! It's bad! We need to turn the oven cleaning off and get out of the house right away!"

My mom did turn off the cleaning but drew the line at a forced evacuation. "Please, just go to sleep and stop worrying," she said as she shuffled down the hall in her pink slippers and robe.

But that was impossible. And unproductive. My parents and sisters were distracted by their grief and in need of protection. Sure, they hid their grief fairly well—hardly anyone talked about Mark as we fell back into our ordinary routines. But it was clear to me. My mother took an extra twenty minutes getting to the grocery store in order to avoid passing Mark's grave; tears welled up in my father's eyes whenever he watched the Celtics win a game, with an empty seat beside him; and my sisters were hardly ever around, always at their friends' houses.

As the stone—as the person capable of being one—the job of keeping them safe fell to me. I'd let Mark down; I couldn't fail again.

I spent a lot of nights thinking about death. Mostly, I considered the oldest people in my life: my grandparents, my father. I looked at them and thought they appeared too fragile, so vulnerable, as if they needed my protection and love in a way others seemingly less at risk—my sisters, even my mother— didn't quite.

But I also thought about my own death. Sunday School taught me that we have a soul that lives on, though our bodies are buried in the ground. I wondered about the mind, though. Would it live on like my spirit, or disintegrate slowly in time, like flesh? Neither seemed likely. What seemed most probable, and most frightening—what made death itself as scary as it was—was my suspicion that the mind went out as swiftly as a candle is snuffed, as completely as a spider devoured by a Venus fly trap.

It was that vanishing, the sudden snuff of the flame, that haunted me most; the sad sense of eternity we lived with every day an illusion, like the light we see from stars long gone.

The only thing I could do was train my mind to be prepared.

I knew there was no way to be physically ready for *anything*, but it was important to try—to wrestle with each fear; to pick it up, spin it around, and toss it like a shot-put into space.

I tried prayer, too. The prayers started simply—"God, please take care of Mark up there, and please keep the rest of my family safe, healthy, and happy here on earth." I soon decided that I should probably include my friends. Or more broadly, "everyone I care about." That was selfish, though, to consider only those *I* cared about, so I added: "And everyone in the whole world, even though I know that's not really possible, but please, God, please try to keep as many people as possible safe, healthy, and happy." I listed as many relatives and friends as I could think of before moving on to my prayers of forgiveness.

"I'm sorry, I know I've asked you for a lot, but please forgive me. For all the bad things I've ever done, whether I realized they were bad or not, because sometimes I do bad things but don't realize they're bad until I think about them afterwards. Please forgive me for all the bad things I think, too, because I can't always control it. I know it's no excuse, and that I should try, but I do try, and will try harder. I promise. Just please forgive me for all the bad thoughts that pass through."

This took hours. Between these tailored prayers, I recited

the "Our Father"—mostly in my mind, though sometimes aloud if that seemed necessary. I made the sign of the cross. Three times in a row, for the Trinity. Then three sets of three. Then three sets of three sets.

Sometimes I fell asleep midway through a three-sets-of-three-sets kind of night, and all the better, because other times I finished all of them still wide awake, with no hope of falling asleep.

In some ways, it was sheer and utter torture, but necessary—the least I could offer to God, if he would just keep the remaining members of my family safe. And healthy.

Happy was a plus I could worry about later.

Chapter Five
Two Weeks Later

"One year has passed since that darkest of days, and yet it seems like only yesterday."

Tangled among rumpled sheets and blankets, I awake to the matter-of-fact voice of the Channel 8 news reporter. I glance over my shoulder at the television, and there it is: the burning tower. The plane hitting the one behind it, setting it, in turn, ablaze, amassed in an ever-expanding billow of smoke.

I snap the power off and reach up to tap the computer mouse, which is two feet away from the bed, to check my instant messenger. Nothing. No word from anyone . . .

It is Andy I am hoping to hear from. Why? Because he said he would get in touch with me. He said he wanted to hang out. We agreed it was an . . . awkward night, and he apologized. He seemed to mean it. He seemed to mean all of it.

I glance at the time on my alarm clock—fifteen minutes until my first class, The American Political Party System. I dress and dash across campus as fast as my legs will carry me.

"So much of the strength of the United States as a nation depends on its two-party system."

This, the voice of Professor Baxter—a tall and lovely woman with a singsong voice, who can't be a day over 35. I've been doodling interlocking diamond patterns—I've nearly filled the entire white portion at the top of my notebook page—when I hear this declarative sentence and look up.

"A multiparty system, in which as many as five or more parties exert serious influence, often leads to chaos and radicalism, where citizens tout their party affiliations as though they were of a sports team, or a favorite band—they spray-paint the name of the party in alleyways, they rally in the streets when they win . . ."

So polarities work . . . I scribble on the page. *Polarities = balance?*

A political party as sports team . . .

Always a question mark or ellipsis. It would be nice to be certain of something for a change. Like this professor—certain enough of the two-party system's superiority to advocate for it in a classroom full of impressionable students. I mean, it's admirable, that type of conviction, that certainty; the unequivocal way in which she presents her stance. It's what I need to cultivate myself.

But I'm starting to fear that it's just not in me.

On my first day of class as a political science major last year, the professor, Dr. Reichler, asked what everyone's "political experience" was. I squirmed and silently panicked as I heard about this classmate's internship with that senator, another's efforts while volunteering for a presidential campaign, and one student with a family full of mayors, selectmen, congressmen—name-drops that meant nothing to me but drew flashes of recognition and follow-up questions from the teacher.

It was an intro class. I had no political experience—just an interest in global dynamics and "current events," along with a vague desire to wend my way inside of them—to play some part, large or small, in positive change. When it came my turn to speak, because I had nothing to lose, I said the truest thing that entered my mind: "My only political experience is growing up working in my father's diner, where farmers and businessmen, rich and poor, all sat at the same counter, reading the same newspapers, spouting their views as they ate the same eggs and drank the same coffee."

The tweed-suited teacher smiled and seemed gratified by the answer. At the time, I felt triumphant—at the very least, my answer stood out and seemed creative. But as time passes, that smile has lingered in my mind, and I've come to see it for what it was: the teacher thought I was cute, the way a child is cute when she is too old to believe in Santa but still does; she will grow out of this stage some day and see the folly of her thinking—the absurdity of her belief—but for now, to him—and for his benefit, not mine—it was simply a charming and refreshing expression of innocence.

I know I don't belong in this major anymore, with these people who have an actual future in the field. They aren't here with some romantic notion of examining the word *politics* as if under a microscope, or to figure out why "world peace" can't exist, or if that's even necessarily true. They probably already know these things, in a way that will take me years to comprehend; they are here practicing to be lawyers, politicians, leaders.

Even my English classes are like that—filled with kids who probably heard the same advice I did, that future lawyers sometimes major in English because the attention to language is relevant, useful. I use that reason myself when my family asks why I chose English as a double major with Poli-Sci. "It would be good for law school, if I decide to go. And there's journalism, marketing—lots of fields use English."

At least that's what I tell them. But what I really want to do is get lost in words and books; in the poetry of, say, William Blake, and maybe find my way out by the end of my four years.

It's an incredibly impractical way to behave, but I can see no other.

I'm looking forward to my next class today, a creative writing workshop. The task in that course is to write ten pages per week toward a book project of each student's choosing. The first assignment, which I completed last night, is an introduction—a sort of statement of intent. I stayed up late, first trying to get into the mindset to write. I made it ceremonial: I lit a jasmine-scented candle, played some bluegrass music, lay down on my bed, shut my eyes, and breathed in deep. *Turn each thought into a cloud, and watch it float away,* I told myself, as I'd learned to do in high school Health class, and it felt silly, but it worked. I started to feel in tune with the elements around me. Even simple objects—my lamp, my socks—somehow took on a life.

After precisely ten minutes—I kept track—of trying to empty my mind, I stood and performed some stretches. When I finally sat at the computer to write, my fingers tapped rapidly at the keys, sensing around for words as if I were a piano player conjuring the next note, thoughts flowing faster than I could capture them on the screen; they were thoughts I didn't understand but was prepared to spend the whole semester trying to unravel. At the top of the page, I wrote, "If there is a way, then I am here to find it. If there is no way, then I am here to make it."

I'm slightly embarrassed to turn it in; it feels so transparent, like an x-ray scan of my soul. Part of me hopes that the professor will see how badly I want this; will discover a hint of life in here and help me draw it out. Right now, that feels worth the exposure.

"Okay, everyone. We'll pick this up next time." Professor Baxter's words are followed instantly by the requisite rumble of notebooks closing, books being shoved into bags, chairs screeching backward, and students filing out noisily from the room. I pack up my things, too, and speed off toward the student union, to buy my mid-morning banana.

But on the way there, about halfway down the sidewalk that cuts through the quad—a large, grassy area between three classroom buildings and the student center—I see the solitary figure of a man who, from this distance, appears to be none other than Andy.

I walk forward, adjust my shoulder bag so it won't bunch up my shirt, whip back the wisps of my hair, and brush my eyebrows straight with my fingers. As we draw nearer to one another, I confirm that it is, in fact, Andy, who now unavoidably sees me, too, and waves with a faint smile. "Hey," he calls. His walking slows, then stops.

"Hey," I say, attempting a casual smile.

"How are ya?" He runs his fingers through his wavy hair and looks up at the clouds.

"Not bad, not bad," I say, nodding compulsively.

"Good." He nods, too. "Well, I gotta get to class. But hey. We should hang out soon."

He wants to see me again, I think. *He* is *a good guy* . . .

"Yeah, we should." My voice is too quick, too high, too loud; much too loud, like I'm shouting. "I gotta run, too. Take care."

"See ya," he says, as I hurry away and he walks in the opposite direction.

My body—my hands, my knees, the entirety of my skin—vibrates as I move, and I release the breath I've been holding. *Banana,* I think. *Need a banana.* Just then, something else—my cell phone—begins to vibrate, startling me. I don't recognize what it is at first. Then, I pull it from the front pouch of my backpack and read the name, *STEVE,* in all caps through the cover.

How does he know?

Not now. Now is not the time for him.

I push the button to stop the vibrating, but it begins again a moment later. "Hello?" I answer.

"Rinie." His voice sounds urgent.

"What is it?"

"Are you okay?"

"Yes, yes. Why wouldn't I be okay?"

"You didn't return my calls yesterday. I was worried something was wrong."

I don't remember seeing any calls. Yesterday itself is like a blur of color and sound. "What would be wrong?"

"Don't know, I was just worried."

"About what? What did you think could be wrong?"

"Wasn't sure. That's why I called again."

I shake my head and rub my eyes. "Everything's fine. I think. . . . Is everything fine?"

Steve chuckles. "Silly. That's what I'm asking you!"

"Well," I say, and pause; my vibrating body stills. "You scared me."

"I'm sorry." His voice is gentle. "Didn't mean to scare you. Everything's okay."

I bite down hard on the words. Steve has a way of frightening me that I can't explain or understand, and not for lack of trying. It's like he knows something is looming, something that could destroy me; he holds this awareness like a delicate flower intolerant of light. "Okay," I say.

But a dark, gray sense that everything is farthest from okay has settled in. What's coming my way? What is happening right now that will sneak up on me in some terrible way beyond my control?

The air hangs steady, not the slightest breeze; I look around and see the quad mostly deserted of people. The church bells chime four times—*ding, dong, ding, dong*—the first ding and dong higher-pitched than the second, which I recognize as the first section of a four-part song; I hear in my mind the missing crescendo that's supposed to follow, which makes me aware of— the time. "Shit! I'm late for class. Gotta go. I'm sorry."

"No problem. Call me later, okay?"

"Why?"

He laughs again. "Because I want to talk to you, silly. Jeez."

"Okay."

Though I don't want to speak to him anymore—we're broken up, and broken-up people are not supposed to talk. "Or you call me." *Why did I say that?* "But I gotta go."

I'm fifteen minutes late to class. Professor Snyder glares at me when I try to slip into the room. "Welcome," she says. "Everyone has turned in their work." She holds up a stack of papers. "Please do so."

"I'm sorry," I say, as I dash to my seat.

I untangle myself from my bag, finger through folders, books, and stray papers to find the two-page introduction I printed out last night. No one speaks or moves; I've now got an audience. "Here it is."

I rush to the front of the room and turn in the assignment. Professor Snyder takes my pages with a free hand and tosses them onto the table behind her while she holds the rest in her hands.

Puzzled, I stand immobile and gaze at her dumbly.

She returns my blank look, then faces the rest of the class. With a smile, the professor declares, "It's vital that we're all on time for class. It's disrespectful not only to me but to your fellow classmates when we're late."

For a split second—the kind that allows for irrational thought—I want to respond and say that it's also disrespectful to toss people's work—practically their heart and soul—aside, onto a table, as though it were no more than trash. But I take a deep breath and think, *You're the one who is disrespectful.*

"Now, let's move on."

That evening, after a swim at the gym, I stop at the dining hall and squeeze through the rush-hour crowd to buy my dinner of cucumber-and-carrot sushi rolls. When I get back to the dorm, I take a long, hot shower, and sit up on my bed, in front of my computer. It's Thursday night. A going-out night at college. Perfectly feasible, when Andy said—again—"we should hang out soon," that *soon* might mean *tonight.*

I pick up a sushi roll and finger out half the rice, then pop the roll into my mouth. I open my instant messenger's buddy list and consider writing him. Why not? I saw him today; we'd been friendly. He'd just said he wanted to hang out.

So I type, "Hi," and press send.

I wait two minutes for a response. To distract myself, I open my music player and create a playlist. I eat another sushi roll and poke out the cucumbers from the rest to eat only those. I toss the remains, and—after adding twenty songs to my playlist, and still seeing no response—power off my computer monitor. I put on my slippers, leave the room, walk down the hall, and knock on the open door of the room where Daniella lives with her roommate, Jasmine.

Of everyone on the floor, I feel most comfortable with Daniella. Whenever I see her in the common room, she's warm and friendly, but in a low-key way. She mostly keeps to herself, yet makes easy little gestures, like inviting me to join her for dinner in the cafeteria or on a trip to the convenient store to buy laundry soap.

We aren't exactly best friends, and yet she is the closest

black friend I've ever had. The only, really; my entire high school class did not include one black female.

"Come in," Daniella calls, when she hears me knock. "What's up?"

"You doing anything tonight?"

She glances about her room. "No plans, really. You have something in mind?"

"I'm in the mood to go out."

Daniella laughs and smoothes the fabric of her bedspread. "Damn, girl. You're getting into the party spirit here, huh?"

I grin. "Yes. I want to go dancing." The moment I say this, my cheeks burn red. I *do* love to dance, but now I think of the stereotype, of black people liking to dance, and I fear that I've offended her, that it came out all wrong.

She throws her head back in a laugh. "Ehh . . . I could do some dancing tonight. I'll call Jasmine and see if she wants to come."

In relief, I breathe, "Good. I'll get ready."

The three of us, dressed for a night out, down a shot of Bacardi 151.

"Perfect college-girl drink," Daniella explains as she pours a second round. "Gets you drunk fast and cheap."

"Sounds good to me," I say. I gulp it down, wipe my mouth, and cough immediately. "Ugh. I've never tasted anything like that."

"Because there *is* nothing like that," Jasmine says. "It's practically moonshine."

I like the sound of that, moonshine. We leave the apartment and head out into the darkness while I let the word filter through me like plasma. I throw my hands into the air as we move onward and then spin in a forward spiral motion, shouting, "Moonshine!"

The girls are amused.

We board the subway. From the pitch-black night, descending into sharp fluorescent lighting, we're like astronauts on a return trip breaching earth's atmosphere. There are no seats, so we stand and grip a metal pole. I look around at all the silent people, seated side by side, on orange-colored benches in rows facing one another, feet planted to the sticky rubber floor. Girls cluster wearing miniskirts, spiky heals, skin-tight tube tops, their eyes caked with bright-colored shadow, lips stark red and glossy. The guys are gathered together as well, in their collared, button-down shirts with jeans and dress shoes. It's a middle school dance at the start of the night—girls on one side, boys on the other. All of them will eventually grow into their outfits and makeup, drink by drink, throughout the evening, but for right now it seems they're simply holding their collective breaths.

And then there's us—already drunk, with that wild-eyed look and wobbly stance. I start laughing senselessly.

"Someone's got the giggles," Daniella says.

This makes me laugh harder. Ordinarily, I would feel the need to stifle and silence myself, but I'm too drunk and free to care; the laughing is rapturous.

I can sense eyes watching me, glancing at me sideways while I laugh on and on. I grip a pole and allow my body to sway with the train as it takes each turn. *It's only 9 p.m.*, their looks seem to say. *Much too early for that.* But I don't even care.

We exit at the Harvard Ave T stop and walk down the block to a bar called O'Malley's. One of the first people we see is Agnes, who's standing with a group of three girls I don't know. She sips her drink and saunters over with them.

"Hi!" I say, waving and smiling.

Looking only at Daniella, with enough of a smile to suggest

she might be kidding, she says, "What are you bitches doing here?"

Daniella rolls her eyes. "Back off, Agnes."

"I'm serious. What're you doing here?"

"Get a drink and cool off, girl," Daniella says. "This place is open to the public." She brushes past Agnes, then says, "Come on, Rinie."

That's when Agnes's eyes set on me.

It's eerie, the way she's staring—like she wants me to know that she's watching me—but I'm able to cast it off quickly after we stop to buy a round of drinks. I order a Jack and Diet, and then we make our way to the dance floor.

The dance floor feels like a safe place for me to come alive, to let sound waves and rhythm translate into motion.

Jasmine and Daniella, I soon see, also love to dance. We move in a small circle together, and yet I feel perfectly alone, as if each of us is dancing within a neighboring bubble, a confined and comfortable space of freedom from the surrounding chaos. I'm weightless, swimming under water and somehow able to breathe, every joint and muscle in my body responding fluidly to each cadence and slope in the music's tone.

After a few songs, the DJ halts the music to announce some sort of dance-off.

I cup my hands around my mouth and shout to the girls, "I'm going to pee!"

I wriggle my way through the mass of people, gazing straight ahead, careful not to make eye contact with anyone. Fully inebriated now, I feel superhuman, fierce, determined to control my every action. So when a large man in a tight black T-shirt and bulging muscles obstructs my path, smiles, and then shouts, "Can I buy you a drink?" I respond immediately with a loud, "No, thank you!" and keep pushing past.

"What?" he yells, tapping my shoulder.

"I said, no! No, thank you!" and I smile.

That's the way, I think—*polite, but firm.*

The man lowers his eyes, reaches out and grabs my plastic cup. He squeezes it hard, the liquid pours out over the sides and onto my hand, then he smashes it onto the ground. "Bitch!" he yells.

I jump back, shocked in place, and stare at him for a moment before it occurs to me to *move.*

I make a beeline back to where Jasmine and Daniella have resumed their dancing.

"We have to go!" I shout. "I'm sorry, but let's go. Let's go somewhere else."

"What? Why?" Daniella calls back.

"There's a guy here, he smashed my cup. We gotta go."

Together, we weave our way off the dance floor and out of O'Malley's to where a large and boisterous crowd now trails down the sidewalk waiting to get in. "What the hell?" Jasmine yells, her head rolling backward. "Where's the fire?"

"There was this guy . . ." I say, my body trembling, "He wanted to buy me a drink and I said no, and then he grabbed my cup and threw it down and I . . . I thought he was going to come after me."

"Eh, fuck him." Daniella waves her hand. "Those men in there are crazy sometimes."

I look up at the dark sky, feeling awful. "I'm sorry I made you guys leave."

Jasmine clicks her tongue and says, "Don't even worry about it. It was time to go, anyway. Like D said, that place was getting crazy. Besides, it's only 1:15. We've got plenty of time to hit up another bar."

We decide on The Den, which has a live band every Thursday night. "Three of us," Jasmine says to the bouncer. She holds out a twenty-dollar bill for the five-dollar cover charge and points to Daniella and me.

He glances at each one of us and says, "Sorry. Too close to last call."

"We don't mind paying," Jasmine says. "We just want to have one drink."

"We're not letting anyone else in." He crosses his arms over his chest and turns his attention to the crowd in the bar.

"What?" Daniella chimes in. "What're you talking about? It's not even 1:30. This place closes at 2."

"We're not letting anyone else in."

"Dude, that's bullshit." Jasmine pricks the air with a finger like she's popping a balloon with a knife. "You're always letting people in up to the last minute."

"Not tonight." His eyes remain fixed on the crowd.

Daniella, who's also surveying the room, taps my arm, then shouts, "Rinie, look!" She points toward the mob in the center of the bar. "It's Andy! Isn't that Andy? The guy you hooked up with?"

My knees feel as if they'll betray me at any moment and give out. "Shh!" I hiss.

"That's him! Isn't that him?" She's still pointing, very obviously, and I try to look anywhere but in that direction. To the bouncer, she says, "We know those people. We want to hang out with our friends in there. You gotta let us in."

"Nope." He still won't look at us. "Sorry."

Part of me is thankful, but another part of me wants to storm in and grab Andy by the shoulder, swing him around, and yell, "What am I, a joke to you? What am I, a *jerk*?"

"That's bullshit," Jasmine says. "Come on, let's go. We don't need this shit-hole."

Outside, when we gather on the sidewalk to strategize, I say, "I don't understand. I've never seen a bouncer turn someone away this early." I am a little disappointed; I would at least have liked to see Andy's reaction to my standing there in front of him. I'd have liked to say, "How's now for hanging out?"

Jasmine rolls her eyes. "Get used to it, honey. You're hanging out with black girls now."

"What?" I shake my head no. "That can't be why he wouldn't let us in."

"Yes," Daniella says, "it can be, and it is. Rinie, this is Boston, and you're hanging out with black girls. That's just what it is."

"Fuck Boston!" Jasmine screams into the night. "This would never happen in New York or Miami. Fuck Boston!"

A group of girls across the street, blonde hair glowing under the streetlamp, turn to stare in our direction.

"What you looking at?" Jasmine yells. "Nothin' to see here, *folks!*" She laughs wildly. "Never seen a *black* person before?"

The girls seem horrified and turn away, and I imagine a former version of myself retreating along with them; a version that I pity and am happy to have shed.

Back on campus, we aren't ready to go home yet. "Let's find a party in the townhouses," Daniella says. "Luckily, we have *this*." She grins and then removes a silver flask from her pocket.

"You've been holding out on us!" Jasmine says. "Give me that." She grabs the flask and takes a swig. "Here." She hands it to me, and I look at Daniella.

"Go ahead!" she urges. "Let's keep this party going." So I take a long swig of what I know, from the sting, is straight vodka.

As we make our way through the village of townhouses, we give up on the prospect of finding a party—it's much more fun to travel through the paths in the darkness, dancing on the pavement to the music blaring from the windows and drinking from the flask.

One group of houses, at the farthest end of the row, is playing the loudest music of all—an infectious tune by the band Outkast, called "Bombs over Baghdad." The three of us sing and laugh and spin around grooving our shoulders to the beat. I throw my head back and glimpse the source of the music, where a large American flag drapes down from a window. It's held by a guy who pumps his fist in the air and yells, "Yeah!" in our direction as we dance.

That is when I really hear the lyrics: "Bombs Over Baghdad."

YOU COULD BE NEXT.

The words appear in my mind—from an article I read online, about bombs and leaflets being dropped from US military planes. One, with a warning: NO TRACKING OR FIRING ON THESE AIRCRAFT WILL BE TOLERATED. YOU COULD BE NEXT.

This, I think—the blasting of the song, the waving of the flag—is an ugly celebration of destruction and war. Which I'm complicit in.

The song itself, and its intentions—who knows what they are. But these guys, waving their flag from the window, shouting, "USA"—

I stop dancing and stand there in a daze for a moment, then walk forward. The other girls follow, until we reach our building.

"One more shot before bed," Daniella announces as we

step off the elevator and onto our floor.

Why not, I think. *Fuck it.*

"Tonight was a riot," Jasmine says when we're back in the dorm.

"Sure was," Daniella agrees, "except that asshole bouncer at The Den. But hey, how about seeing Andy, Rinie? How about that!"

The room—already spinning—now picks up speed. "Whadda you mean?"

"I just mean, we saw Andy! Too bad we couldn't go in. He's one good-looking guy. Way to go, girl. Good for you."

"Whadda you mean?" I repeat. I place my hands on the counter to steady myself on the stool.

Daniella laughs. "What do you mean, what do I mean? I'm saying, that was one damn fine, quality hookup. And my favorite part is that Agnes was *so pissed!*" Daniella slaps her knee.

I bite my lip hard. "Agnes was pissed?"

Daniella waves a hand. "Oh yeah, but that's Agnes for you. Drama queen. She acted like she was all pissed because she had to walk home alone that night. That you *let* her walk home alone. Ha! As if she didn't do that all the time! She just has a crush on him, and she's jealous." She leans in toward me. "I'm talking *major* crush. *Major* jealous."

These words tear through me. "Oh my God, I had no idea," I breathe.

Daniella laughs again. "Don't you even worry about it. It's fine. In fact, it's awesome! That girl needs to get a little stirred up every once in a while. It's good for her."

Daniella's voice fades to the background and the sentence *You let her walk home alone* blinks in my mind like a flashing neon sign.

"Have you heard from him at all?" Jasmine asks. "Andy, I mean."

"Um, not really . . ."

"That doesn't surprise me," Daniella waves. "Don't get me wrong, you're cute and all, but guys like that . . . they don't call."

"No, they do not," Jasmine nods.

"They don't get as serious as all that. Not yet. Not until they go home to their yuppie little suburbs and find their perfect All-American beauty queen with the fellow blue-blood parents. Innocent and pure—yeah right, but they can believe the lie because they went to different colleges and the stories stayed there."

"It's true," Jasmine adds. "Anyway, you're too ethnic-looking for a guy like that." She places a hand on mine. "And I mean that in a good way!"

Major crush . . . yuppie little suburbs . . . blueblood parents . . . ethnic-looking . . .

I grip the countertop and stand, accidentally flipping my stool to the floor. "I gotta go to bed."

"Sweetie, don't you worry about a thing." Daniella wraps her arms around me in a hug; I'm stiff as cardboard. "This was a great night!"

I manage a tiny smile and say, "Thank you for coming out with me. You too, Jasmine."

Jasmine waves. "Any time!"

I stagger off down the hall to my room, where I sit on the edge of the bed and stare at my computer. I click on Andy's name and type, "Fuck you," into the message box, but then delete it. "Fuck *you*," I whisper loudly and punch myself in the leg. "Fuck *you*."

I lie on my back, dig my nails into the sheets, and focus on the ceiling, trying to steady the room. My insides swoosh into a wild stream, bursting upward and storming out of my body in a heave. I heave and heave until no more liquid emerges and I feel emptied entirely.

"Rinie?"

It's Kathryn's quiet voice that breaks the silence.

I attempt to say, "Yeah," but it comes out fleshy and muted.

"Rinie, you okay?"

I clear my throat enough to say, "Yes," and add, hoarsely, "I'm sorry."

Kathryn shifts out of bed, switches on her desk lamp, and ambles over to my side of the room. "Oh my God! You puked all over your bed!"

My head is just slightly raised above the pillow, avoiding the vomit. I can do nothing but wince.

"I'll get you some water and a bucket, but try to sit up."

She is wearing blue paisley jammies. Clean and soft as they brush against my bare arm, they make her seem eons away from where I am. She turns before walking out of the room and adds, "You could've choked on all that."

When she returns, she manages to ball up the sheets and stuff them into a plastic garbage bag, then spreads a clean sheet over the bed, while I make a feeble, pointless effort to assist, but all I can do is roll from side to side as she slides them out from under me.

"I don't know how to thank you," I slur, dazed and ill now more from the violence of the purging than the drinks.

"Don't worry about it." She sits in the chair beside my bed. "But listen, you can't sleep on your back. You need to sleep on your side. You can die puking in your sleep like that." She shakes her head like a mother in disbelief. "What has gotten into you?"

"What do you mean?"

It stuns me to hear her ask this; I do feel changed, but I

didn't expect anyone to notice.

"You seem different. Kind of like, out of control. And then there was that night you slept out . . . not that it's a big deal, but it surprised me. You didn't seem like that kind of girl when I first met you."

It's as if she's reached inside my chest and plucked the taut string of an achy nerve. The dual relief and pain sets me sobbing. "I didn't think I was that kind of girl, either, but I guess I am."

"Listen, there's nothing wrong with it, as far as I'm concerned. If anything, I was impressed. I thought you seemed a little . . . overly virginal when we first met. But yeah, I can see something's been . . . "

Words rush out of me in a torrent, like the vomit did earlier. "I don't have a fucking clue *who* I am anymore. I don't know what I'm doing here. I don't fit in and I have no friends and my grandma died and I miss my brother who would hate me right now and my boyfriend moved away and I broke up with him but he keeps calling me and I keep picking up the phone because I'm an *asshole*." I slap at my tears. "I tell him I don't want to be with him, but I pick up the damn phone anyway because I'm too scared to be alone and . . . "

Kathryn grips my right arm and shouts over me, "Rinie, Rinie, stop, I don't know what you're talking about . . ." but I keep on ranting.

"And that night I didn't come home? I slept with a guy. I didn't even know him." My breathing grows rapid and thin. "I didn't mean to, I really didn't. We were kissing and I told him I didn't want to have sex with him, and I honestly believed that was all I had to do is just say it. How could I be so *stupid!*" And I punch myself so hard in the leg this time that, even in this drunken haze, I know I'll see a bruise in the morning.

"Wait," Kathryn says, her tone shifting. Still holding my

arm, she sits beside me on my bed. "Rinie, what are you saying?"

I pull my arm away from her and punch the bed. "But I still hate him!" I begin yelling, in a voice I have no control over, "I hate him! I hate him! I hate him!" My throat burns from the purging and shouting.

Kathryn grips my cheeks and forces me to look her in the eyes. "Rinie, calm down. What exactly are you saying?"

"I told him we couldn't have sex. I *told* him."

She lets go of my face, now, and stands. "Wait, what?"

I stare down at my lap, my head shaking from side to side as if to say *no,* over and over again. "But he just like forced his way into me. I should have kicked his fucking ass off of me." I kick the desk in front of me and hear the loud clang of metal.

Kathryn stands now, her voice growing louder and sharper. "Rinie. You were *raped.*"

"What?" I shake my head as if to wake myself up. "No, that's not what I meant to say."

"But that's what you *are* saying, Rinie. It's rape."

"No, that's not what I meant." I try to sober myself, to explain more clearly.

Kathryn cocks her head to the side and spits out each word as if angry at it. "It's called date rape, Rinie. Welcome to the 21st century. That's what it is."

CHAPTER SIX
THE HIGH SCHOOL YEARS

It had been a strange summer, that one before high school—it was the first time I'd been to Greece or seen my grandparents on that side in four years. After Mark died, we cancelled our trip; the first summer of my life we didn't go. In the following years, my parents decided that my sisters were old enough to make the trip alone. They always asked if I wanted to join them, but each time, I declined, though I did, very badly, want to go. I wanted to see the village, the rocks, the animals, the mountains, the water—and that soft, yellow light enveloping all of it.

To get there, though, meant flying across the Atlantic; careening through the chaotic streets of Athens; riding the ferry over to the island; driving along the cliff roads while we crammed ourselves with our oversized luggage into the death-trap of a tiny rental car. Too much uncertainty for my brain to process, too much risk and fear for me to mitigate with my nightly rituals and prayers.

The night before the trip, I talked to God.

God had been hiding from me in those days. Maybe it was because I used his name too often: "God, please keep my family safe, healthy, and happy," "God, please forgive me for my sins." In Sunday School, we'd learned about Yahweh—which meant "I am who am," a phrase that confused me so much that it burrowed a permanent place for itself in my consciousness, popping up every once in a while like a Jack-in-the-box assert-

71

ing itself. The ancient Jews weren't supposed to say the word too many times, out of respect for the name's power—and yet there I was every night, saying *God,* over and over.

As a small child, I thought God was the plumpish man with the salt-and-pepper beard and sand-colored suit who came into our Sunday School class every week with an envelope we threw our quarters into as dues. Our teacher had said that the church was God's house, and this man—whose official, earthly name was Mr. Papadopoulos—was always there; he seemed to live there. We paid our money to God for the time spent in his house.

God wasn't so different from Santa Claus. You had to be good for him, too, or you wouldn't get your presents. Sometimes it seemed even more important to be good for Santa, because his gifts were the ones you could actually see.

In the third grade of Sunday School, the teacher had said that God was in all the things we loved, in all the things beautiful and right. That made more sense. God, for me, was everywhere, but most especially in Minos. The beauty of the earth was nowhere more present to me than in that sand, that dust and rock, those open fields with the sunlight beaming through the brush, or in the dark, thick waves as I swam in the ocean.

But even though I tried to speak with God daily in those years after Mark died, I wasn't sure he ever heard me. I couldn't feel him at all. I spoke to him in frantic hums, the same words whispered and thought, whispered and thought, until they held no meaning at all. So on that night before my first trip back, I took a new approach—I'd recited enough of those same prayers to last a lifetime, and I needed something else, something more; to know if he was really out there; to know if this world was really good, and could be trusted. *Please, God, give me a sign,* I implored. *Either way, give me a sign.*

During takeoff, I clutched a silver cross in my right fist and clenched my jaw so tightly that it ached. If my family noticed, they spared me any teasing or questions of concern.

But we made it into the air, and an hour into the flight, I remained calm enough to read and comprehend more than one full sentence in my book. Soon, the pages flipped by, my mind wandered into the story, my limbs relaxed, and I even fell asleep.

When I awoke, though, it was to a terrible thud, as if the belly of the plane had thunked down on some sort of ground in the sky. The cabin banked from left to right, the plane swooped down and up, and frantic murmurs spread through the waking crowd. The lights, which had been toned down for all to sleep, flicked on to full brightness, and the seatbelt and "no smoking" signs lit up and blinked. My mother looked like she was having a tooth pulled as she gripped her armrests, pushing down so hard as if to raise herself and the entire plane up.

"Are we okay?" Eugenia said.

"I'm going to be sick," Vicky groaned.

My father, four seats away from where I sat by the window, slit open his resting eyes to say, "It's fine. Just a little bumpy."

With my head leaned back, I felt remarkably at ease. This was it: the sign, the moment of truth, and I understood that phrase in a new way then—it was time to pay attention, because truth of this sort, of the life-and-death variety, can only reveal itself in these infinitesimal moments of clarity. Anything beyond that is more than we, or it, can bear.

None of my fears mattered anymore. *If this is the end,* I thought, *well at least I won't have to worry anymore.*

But we made it to Athens and the island and the village in one piece, and I had heavy thanks to pay for that fact.

The village looked basically the same as I remembered. Yet something important had changed—the once-charming broken rocks along the path just looked old and in need of repair; dangerous, even. My grandparents' house, which at one time seemed like a cave carved into the mountainside, had gained a definite shape, no longer blending into the landscape. The coat of blinding radiance was gone.

When we arrived at their house, I kissed Yiayia and Pappou politely on both cheeks and said hello, how are you. During dinner, I felt too shy to speak; my skills in Greek had grown rusty from lack of use, and I feared sounding silly, feared starting a thought and not being able to finish it. Yiayia laughed lightly at my silence and said, "What, are you a stranger now?" And then, reassuring herself, and me, she added, "Oh, I know. You'll open more. *Se xero,* I know you."

But Pappou returned my silence, as he always had.

"But I couldn't come back all those years!" I wanted to say. "Believe me, I wanted to, but I couldn't!"

I didn't have the words, though, to explain all this. I wished I were like an animal, able to communicate through waves and instinct, through physical presence and an unselfconscious awareness of how much truth can pass silently between two bodies of life. Instead, I felt distinctly adult, emptied of all wonder, intent solely on getting what I wanted—in this case, to be left alone, outside the discomfort. Our connection in the past had been like a wink in the darkness—but now, I wanted all such mysteries gone.

So I left Greece that summer quietly and unobtrusively. As the time to say goodbye neared, I drifted away from the scene and lingered on the stone steps beside the donkey Calypso's stable, because I didn't know what sort of goodbye to offer this man—and this place—that I suddenly felt I barely knew; that barely knew me.

On the plane ride home, I made a decision. I'd be starting over, at a Catholic high school—a chance for a fresh start. There on the plane, in thought about the school-year ahead, I wrote in my journal, "You know, for once, it would be nice to fit in with a group. Nice to be part of a crowd."

Things had gotten lonely in my orbit in the last few years. My obsessive prayer rituals and worries had taken over my life. Throughout middle school, I'd been friendly enough with anyone nearby, with a few rotating sets of people to eat a quiet lunch with, but there had never been one person I could point to and say, "That's my best friend." No cluster of people to whom I knew that I belonged; with a guarantee that, if the rest of them were gathered somewhere, they'd look around and say, "Hey, where's Rinie? Isn't Rinie coming?" I was tired of being outside of things, feeling like a freak, wondering if others could read my mind—if others could tell that, for instance, in a movie theater, I sat closest to the aisle and screen to ensure a clear path to the fire exits. I was tired of filling my brain with nothing but thoughts of danger.

Plus, I was bored.

So when the first school dance of the year cropped up, it wasn't as difficult as my cousin Mariana might have anticipated when she called and said, "Hold on, you're thinking of *not* going to this dance?" Eugenia, apparently, had told her this news. "Is that *true?*"

Mariana, a sophomore, never missed a dance.

Before I could respond, she said, "You're coming with me"—an order with which I easily complied.

"Okay."

"Wait, really?"

"Sure, why not?"

Mariana and I dressed and prepped at her house that Friday.

"Wear this," she said, as she pulled a blazing-bright pink

75

tank-top from her closet. "That shirt you're wearing . . ." She pointed to my cream-colored blouse with tiny ruffles running along the neckline. "It's more like a shirt you'd wear to the mall or . . . to the library or something."

I rolled my eyes and grabbed the tank top from her hands, then held it up before my chest. "I can't wear this," I said. "It's too bright and . . . too tight."

Mariana sighed like the exasperated parent of a young child. "It's *supposed* to be tight, Rinie. You're in high school now. It's time."

"Time for what?"

"Time for you to start dressing . . . you know, more grown up. More *sexy*." She shimmied her shoulders to indicate *sexy*, and I had to laugh.

"Oh, I'm real sexy!" I said.

"But you *can* be, girl." Mariana appeared genuinely concerned. "I'm serious." She walked over to her bureau and fumbled with her compacts and brushes, then pointed to the shirt in my hands. "Wear that, and I'm going to put some makeup on you, too."

"I can't wear makeup." I took a cautious, sideways glance at the mirror above her bureau, at the dark rings beneath my pale green eyes, my frizzy brown curls, my blotchy tanned skin. "My face will break out."

Mariana put down her blush brush and gawked at me as if I'd announced plans to join a convent. "Rinie, you *have* to wear makeup. *Everyone* wears makeup. You see all those girls who seem like they have perfect faces? Well, they don't. They wear makeup." This I'd heard from my sisters and mom, too. But I wasn't interested in changing the way my face looked and then having to maintain that process forever after, simply to look like myself.

Everything about high school, though, and dances like this,

and what to wear and do at these things, was so new that I relented. "Fine," I said. "I'll wear this. And you can put a little makeup on me, too. But just a little."

Mariana patted her hands together in excitement. "No, no, it will be very natural. I am going to make you look so pretty!"

Half an hour later, we were ready to go. Our parents—all four of them, who planned on piling into Thio Niko's Suburban for the ride to drop us off—were seated in the living room. Upon our entrance, Mariana's mother, Thia Sophia, stood from the couch and said, "Oh my God, look at this! Little Irinie is wearing *makeup! Ftoo, ftoo—*" She pretended to spit, a superstitious gesture intended as a compliment and a way to ward off admiring eyes, then laughed and slapped my father on the knee. "Brother, look at your little girl!"

My father offered an expression of mock-anger "Makeup? No *my* little girl." He stood, pulled me in for a hug, and kissed the top of my head. "You look *beautiful!*" he said, drawing out each syllable in the word, and I curled in my shoulders, wanting to sink through the floor. "Just remember," and he squeezed my shoulder hard, "You my little girl, but you tough. You don't let *anybody* bother you."

The dance was not what I had expected. The only dance I'd ever been to was in my church's community room, with all the lights on, where the DJ played almost entirely Greek music and we circled-danced most of the night to Greek folk songs we learned in the church dance group.

I thought this would feel a lot different, more grand. The lights in the gymnasium were dimmed, but you could still clearly see the pull-out bleachers pushed against the walls, and the black and maroon paint lines drawn across the parquet floor. I'd known that the dance would be held in the gym, but I imagined the space would be somehow transformed, into something mysterious and gallant; something that could explain the starry-eyed look on my siblings' faces when they came home from these dances while I snuck out of bed in my pajamas to greet them at the door.

I stood stiffly between Mariana and her best friend, Maggie, feeling like an ugly plastic doll. What was I supposed to do now? Nobody was dancing. People were standing around in packs, some at least bobbing their heads to the music, but way too many just whispered into each other's ears and then roared with laughter. It was enough to make you think that *you* were the joke.

I cupped my hand over my mouth and called to Mariana, "This is weird."

"What?" she shouted without turning her head as she surveyed the crowd.

"I said, this is weird! What are we supposed to be doing?"

She looked at me, bewildered. "What do you mean? We're hanging out. Hey, Mag. Let's introduce her to some people."

"Sure thing," Maggie said. "Follow me." So we did, as she sauntered over to a group of guys wearing baseball caps and untucked button-down shirts.

"I'd like you to meet my cousin Rinie," Mariana said as we reached them. "Rinie, this is Mark, Dave, Larry, Kevin, and Jack. Guys, she's a freshman."

"A freshman!" one of them whooped. "Welcome to St. Mike's."

I smiled and looked down at my Doc Martin boots. "Thanks."

And that was about it between the boys and me for most of the night. Throughout the dance, Mariana and I hung out, bopping a bit to the music and discussing people's outfits with Maggie. I said hi and waved to some people I recognized from classes. But around 8:30, with less than an hour left, Maggie stalked over to Mariana and me and said, "Girls." She held her hands out as if ready to catch a basketball. "Jack over there is interested in Rinie."

"Ah!" Mariana squealed. "Tell him she's interested, too."

"What?" I hissed. "What are you saying? I don't even remember which one Jack is . . ."

"He's the skinny one in the Mets hat," my cousin said with a quick wave. "But Rinie, he's a *sophomore*. And you're a *freshman*. Besides, saying you're interested is not necessarily saying you *like* the guy and want to be his *girlfriend*."

"But . . ."

"She's right," Maggie said with authority. "Anyway, that's what he wants to know. If you're interested."

Interested? In fact, I was interested . . . mostly to know, in what exactly he was interested. So I shrugged. "Sure, yeah."

"Sure, yeah, what?" Mariana pushed. "You're interested?"

"Yeah," I said dumbly.

Mariana and Maggie released a collective "Eee!"

"Okay," Maggie said. "I'll tell him. Can I give him your number?"

"Yes!" Mariana offered before catching herself. "Sorry. Rinie?"

"Sure."

I smiled a bit in spite of myself—still feeling like a plastic doll, but just a little less ugly.

From that moment on, I became potently aware of that Mets hat: where it went, with whom it spoke, how close it neared to where I stood. So when I discerned it—him—

making way in our direction as the soft opening notes of a slow song came on, my heart beat faster, my shoulders tightened, I drew in my breath and lost all focus. I could hear Mariana speaking words to me as I nodded but couldn't make out a one. "Hello, can you hear me?" she said at last, and then glanced in the angle of my stare. "Oh my God, he's coming over!"

No, I thought. *Please, no.* What do I do? Say?

But there he was, before me in an instant. "Hi," Jack said to me in a low voice. He stared into the brim of his blue baseball cap. "You wanna dance?"

What could I say but "Sure?"

It was "Stairway to Heaven," of course, because why shouldn't it be the longest slow song ever written? Jack cradled his hands loosely around the small of my back. I placed my fingertips lightly on his shoulders and we began to sway, my body awkward and stiff like a wooden plank teetering on its tips.

"Relax," he said in a whisper.

I glanced up at his face and smiled, then looked down quickly, but my body inched toward him a tad, my shoulders loosened and my fingertips curled further over the bones of his shoulder. From there, I could smell the musk of his cologne, and it occurred to me that no boy or man outside my family had ever been this close to me, had ever touched my skin, as he did now, his chin grazing my forehead. While the sound of the harp in the song grew more intense, the whole ceiling of the gym rose higher; his hands on my back slid closer, then past one another, his forearms now pressed into my sides. The crooning voice—"Ooh, and it makes me wonder"—rang out, and my body tensed—I was afraid to alter a step, to twitch, to move in any way outside this precariously comfortable rhythm we'd settled into.

The DJ cut the song off right before the fast part, and Jack and I stood there for a moment—I looking down at my shoes, and he with his eyes set on me. "Well, goodnight," I said, my face tilted downward.

"Goodnight," he said. "Can I call you?"

Yes, I wanted him to call me. *Yes,* I understood a little more now why girls wanted boys to like them, why they wanted to dance with boys. I said, "Sure."

So that's how Jack became my boyfriend, and that's how everything changed. Suddenly, I had so many friends—all these other girls in my grade wanted to know who I was, this freshman girl with a sophomore boyfriend. They invited me to sit with them at lunch, passed me notes, got my number, called me up at night to chat, invited me to their houses after school or to movies and parties.

Grandma called me a "social butterfly," and Mom said things like, "Don't you plan on spending any time at home anymore?" but in a teasing way where I could tell that she was glad. Even my father didn't seem to mind that Jack and I talked on the phone each night, which made me wonder if they'd thought something was wrong with me before.

Jack liked to give me advice about life at St. Mike's—the hidden codes of conduct that I would never have been able to discern on my own, at least not much before my four years there were up. "It all revolves around the football players," he explained. "For whatever reason, to be cool, you need to be friends with the football players. *And . . .*" he paused for effect, "they have a secret language."

This amused me; it seemed so fifth-grade girl. "A secret language?" I said.

"Yes. And it's not really funny, by the way. You'll want to understand it."

"Oh yeah?" I wasn't convinced.

"Yeah. And it changes all the time. They add words and phrases. It's a way of making fun of you without you knowing."

"And why would they care enough to make fun of me?"

"I don't mean you, specifically. I mean anyone. But by the way, you do want them to care enough to make fun of you. If they don't even notice you . . . that's worse."

"How can that be worse? I'd rather they not notice me."

"Rinie, you don't know what you want," he said. "You don't get it yet. But you'll see."

I stored those lines in my brain for later digestion—*You don't know what you want. You don't get it yet*—but moved on and asked for an example.

"Well, like, if they want to call a girl ugly, they'll say *ylgu.*"

"Ugly backward."

"Right, but it's the way they pronounce it. You'd never know, if you didn't *know*. Like *iiillgoo.*"

"I see."

"And black people. They call them *reggins.*"

"What?" Amusement swept away from me like a hat in the wind.

"It's . . . you-know-what, backwards," he explained.

"Right, I got that. But how can they say that? They actually *say* that?"

"Well, yeah. I mean, it's just a joke. It's not like they're actually racist. They even say it to the black guys on the team." He laughed. "All two of them. And those guys think it's funny, too. It's not a big deal."

"Not racist?" My throat tightened, as if clamped by invisible hands. "Then what *is* racist, if that's not?" The words came out a little louder and shriller than I expected.

"Relax, girl. I didn't invent it. And anyway, it's just kidding around stuff. You know."

But I didn't know. I'd never heard anyone, outside of a

book, use that word, and the reason we read those books in the first place was to see how wrong it was to do so.

"Listen, it's better not to get upset about stuff like this," he advised. "You don't want to make enemies in this school. People can be really mean."

"Well, yeah. They can be. That's my point."

"But listen, you're not gonna change that, and you really don't want that meanness directed toward you. It can happen very fast, and then follow you for years. You're only a freshman. You've got too much time to go. I'm only telling you this to try to help you. Not a lot of people are going to say it, but it's a matter of survival."

It seemed so hyperbolic—a matter of survival—until I saw for myself that he was right; after all, survival is about more than just life or death.

In any case, I liked talking to Jack. He opened my eyes to things I didn't understand and thought I probably should. I took for granted sometimes that I was "smart"—smart enough to do fairly well in school without trying too hard. And I was starting to see that taking this for granted could be dangerous. If I rested on it too much—believed too much in my own ability to comprehend—it was more likely that I'd be taken by surprise; I'd rely too much on my own instincts and senses, and then *bam*: the shock of what I didn't know would nail me to the ground.

I could almost see the nails. They were so possible.

But our relationship was mainly confined to the phone. In person, I was shy. In person, there was the threat of kissing, touching, and now that I was in high school, even more than just kissing and touching, and I felt too many years behind the curve. In middle school, being *with* the curve meant having a boyfriend but just talking on the phone and avoiding each other in school, then maybe kissing one monumental day after months of being together, in a prescheduled moment arranged by friends, at a birthday party or school dance. Being ahead of the curve meant more, meant touching, and other things. In high school, this was all ratcheted up even further, and I, who had never had a boyfriend before, was too far behind.

So I started plotting ways out of this boyfriend-girlfriend status. How could I ask him to just be friends? *Simple,* I thought. *Just ask him.* I mustered up the courage and did so all at once.

"But why?" he said. "I don't understand."

"I just . . . think we should be friends." There was no way to tell him the real reason: I was scared to kiss him, *petrified* of sex. I thought of break-up phrases I'd heard on TV. "I feel like I'm not in a good place to have a boyfriend," I said.

He let me off the hook easy: "No problem." It was simple, civil. Done. We'd still talk on the phone every night, and everything important would remain the same.

But the next day in school, word got around quickly. An older girl named Jenny approached me in the cafeteria and said, "What happened with you and Jack?" As if she didn't already know.

"We broke up," I told her. "It was mutual." He had a reputation to maintain, and I wasn't interested in messing that up. I also didn't want the conflict—Jack had taught me well; I didn't need him, or his friends, as enemies.

"That's not what I heard," she said—and, as sad as it is to say, it was a defining moment in my life; one of those nails—"I heard he dumped you because you're a prude." She scrunched up her face in a wince, as if to express sympathy. "And . . . because you're ugly."

I went home that day and looked in the mirror until I saw it: the marbly eyes, the too-flat nose, the rounded face, the frizzy hair, the sideburns, the pimples: Jenny was right. I was ugly.

I'd never thought of myself as *pretty*, though I did kind of like my squinty-eyed smile and the way my hair fuzzed up at the sides in little curls. Growing up, I'd always been called *cute*, which I knew was different from *pretty*. But I never thought I might be *ugly*. It sounded so extreme, somehow worse in its simplicity—deeper and more absolute—than even repulsive or grotesque.

Prude sank in later and didn't bother me much. Though the word was new—I had to ask Mariana to be sure what it meant, which was, "You don't put out. Kind of like a tease, but more like a goody-goody"—the concept was not. In fourth grade, a boy called my house, and my father, in his thick Greek accent, told him, "Don't ever call here again." I hid in my room each night for the rest of the week, embarrassed and ashamed that a boy had called me, and no boy ever called my house again— until Jack.

But ugly stayed with me, and there was nothing I could do about it.

So I didn't even try, from them on. Well, not too much. I did easy, undetectable things to try to make myself more attractive. I read magazines like *Seventeen* and *Cosmopolitan* that offered beauty tips like "Put cucumbers under your eyes at night," or, "Leave conditioner in your hair for a few extra minutes."

From these, I extracted my own insights and rituals. Like pinching my nose for three minutes every morning and night, to try to train it to stay in, to look cute and delicate, like the other girls' noses. I pushed on the hair above my earlobes with my fingertips, training it to stay behind my ears, where it belonged.

I went shopping with Mariana to stores like Aldo Shoes and Contempo Casuals and bought clothes that were cool enough to make me seem "with it," but not trendy enough to stand out. Despite my sisters' insistences, I refused to wear makeup or style my hair. I blow-dried it straight every night, then pulled it back into a ponytail and slept on it to make it flat—God forbid those curls sneak out.

The key was to look as non ugly as possible while not appearing to try at all. Because trying to be pretty and failing was just too much to take. This was the only way I knew to cope, to not keel over from the humiliation of having to walk around that school, and this world, without a bag over my head.

But it's amazing how easily these mean tidbits leaked through.

One night, I was on the phone with a friend named Rachel, who told me, "Listen to this. Mark Fisher and Mikey Miller were talking, and they were saying how you're probably really hairy. Like, you have hair all over you or something. Isn't that so stupid? But don't worry, I defended you. I said, 'Hell no, she's not hairy.'"

I could barely breathe enough to form the question, "Why would they say that?"

"It's stupid, really," Rachel said quickly. "It's probably because you're Greek or something. That Greek people are hairy and so, 'Oh my God, Rinie must be hairy, too,' like—you know, *everywhere*. Since she's Greek." When I said nothing, she continued. "You know how guys are."

That night, horrified, I examined my arms under a lamp. It was winter, and with my summer tan faded, my arms revealed more distinctly the blackness of the hairs. I looked down at my chest and detected a few stray strands between my breasts.

Gross, I thought. *They're right. That is gross.*

The next day, in the grocery store, I begged my mom to buy bleaching cream to lighten the hairs on my arms and belly, and depilatory lotion to remove the faint mustache above my lip. I asked Vicky to pluck my eyebrows, especially the few specks between my eyes, and she was happy to oblige. In school, I analyzed my own complexion and hair against my classmates', noting that mine were darker than almost everyone's—except for maybe Suzan, an exchange student from Lebanon who nobody talked to because she'd once worn leopard print pants on a dress-down day—and I wished for the other girls' milky, silky, blondey softness.

It felt as if I'd awoken from a long, lucid dream. I vowed to get smart. Smarter. After all, I knew how to do this—knew how to prepare for anything.

What might come next? Fat? *Could I be fat?* I started to notice a contour in my hips, my thighs rounded like the top half of an eight. "Those Greek curves," Yiayia had said the summer before. "A little woman's *somataki.*"

It started slowly, with no more mozzarella sticks, no more Doritos, until I ate nothing but steamed broccoli and Special K cereal. My family grew nervous, I could see that. My sisters tried to talk to me, my parents fought about it at night when they thought I was asleep, and I felt bad, especially after all they'd been through—but I only felt bad in my mind, so it didn't matter that much, because my mind I could control. My mind didn't actually *feel.* I was nearing my goal: no feelings at all.

By senior year, I didn't need friends anymore, either. I quit running track and dropped all the clubs and stopped going to parties, events, even classes. Too many times at lunch, my friends said things like "That's all you're eating? An apple?" so I stopped going to the cafeteria and took my breaks in the library. I felt stronger and more focused, safer and calmer, without food and those people. I distanced myself and ate only the amount I deemed necessary to remain steadily ticking between the poles of healthy and sick. Because if I got too sick, my parents would sound the alarm bells and try to send me to more doctors.

But too healthy was too easy, the extra flesh too pacifying. I wanted to feel, to the greatest extent possible, that I could count on myself, on my own bare bones.

The physical emptiness provided a different type of energy. While it became difficult to muster the strength to climb from the first to third floor of the school, I had strength enough in my mind to transcend the daily cares that had gripped me before. I saw more clearly the *temporality* of my experience (I'd learned that dynamite word in English class). These moments were merely raindrops on the ocean of human life. None of it mattered. Everything melded into a blur, and I became conscious of myself as outside of it all. Utterly detached.

Chapter Seven
Late November

I awake to the sound of Kathryn slamming on my snooze button. "Ugh," I mutter, shielding my eyes from the overhead light in our room. "I'm so sorry. What day is it?"

"Tuesday," she calls over her shoulder as she crosses the threshold. "I'm going to class. See you later."

"Tuesday." The clock on my desk reads 10:58 a.m. "Dammit!" I slept through my Political Parties class, and my 11:00 a.m. creative writing course is about to begin.

I jump to my feet and fumble around the room, pulling on pants, stuffing my feet into socks and shoes, washing my face, brushing my teeth, and trying to recall when and how I fell asleep last night.

I'd gotten into bed early, around 10 p.m., hoping that if I began my efforts earlier, I'd manage to drift off to sleep by midnight. But midnight came after a couple hours of reading, deep breathing, sheep counting, and eye straining, and I found myself, still, wide awake. I tried polishing up the chapter due for class, but by 2 a.m., my brain felt scrambled, unable to generate a complete thought or logical sentence. I needed to slow things down, clear out the muck, so I rummaged under my bed for the shoebox where I kept, wrapped in a small plastic bag, among greeting cards from friends and family and random photos, a joint.

I scored this joint earlier in the evening from a guy I knew named Matty, who I ran into at the 7-11 convenient store in Cleveland Circle—I was getting a diet soda; he was there for rolling papers.

We found ourselves in line together and exchanged hellos. On his way out, Matty lingered by the door while I finished paying, then he walked me toward the T. "Look what I got," he said on the way. He held out his hand to display the papers.

"I see," I said with a smile.

"You wanna come by and help us put these to use?"

The thought was immediately appealing. Matty's that rare person I feel comfortable with these days. We met in an Economics class last year—by now, a whole lifetime ago—where we sat next to each other and compared notes before tests. It was a studious friendship, based on a mutually modest dedication to school, which included a simultaneous interest and disinterest in the subject.

So it was disorienting when I encountered him for the first time this year at a party I went to last month with Daniella and Jasmine. He saw me standing alone and came over to say, "What are you doing here?"

I laughed. "Am I not supposed to be?"

"No, no, I didn't mean that. I just didn't think you were the type who . . . partied." He lifted his eyebrows and grinned. "If I knew that, I would have invited you to places sooner."

"I came with my floor-mate, Daniella." I pointed my finger in her direction.

"Nice . . . So, I don't know how *much* you like to party, but I'm about to smoke. Wanna join?"

I nodded. "Sure."

After that, we met a few times for lunch. I drove him to the mall to buy new sneakers, and in return he brought the weed.

So that night, outside the convenient store, faced with the prospect of long, sleepless hours ahead, I agreed to join him.

But as we walked through the door of his apartment, and as he called out "Yo!" to announce his presence and summon his roommates, it turned out they had visitors—Charlie and Andy.

Two months had passed since I'd seen Andy. And yet, he'd been on my mind all too often. In the middle of a class, listening to a lecture about David Hume's "Treatise on Human Nature," or on representations of idolatry in John Milton's "Paradise Lost," all of a sudden I'd wonder, *Why hasn't he called, or written to me online?*

The simple answer, of course, is that he just doesn't care. I don't occur to him. He doesn't like me. If anything, he thinks I am a joke.

These answers don't bother me as much as their implications: I've been a fool to think he would reach out. In his eyes, I'm just some slutty girl he slept with. Why would he think of me as anything more?

Or, maybe he doesn't contact me because he feels guilty. Maybe he feels like a bad person. In this case, I do wish I could help. I wish I could tell him that, really, I do understand, that I've thought about it deeply, all the gray areas, and there are a number of factors at play. First, like all humans, we are both fallible, sinful, prisoners—not just of original sin but also, more concretely, of the circumstances, expectations, and trappings of modern society: He's a guy. He's supposed to get sex from the girl; he's supposed to believe that the lady doth protest too much.

And I. I should have known better. I shouldn't have just "gone with the flow" like that; it wasn't like me at all.

Or was it? And then there's that. Who am I, really, and

what makes me so sure I'm *not* that type? What *is* that type? I didn't even think I was the type who *believed* in "types."

I'm angry, though, too, that he hadn't somehow known that about me. I'm angry with myself for thinking that he could, or would. Or even should.

But he should, I sometimes think. *He should.*

The point is that he's no longer a person in my mind but an idea. So seeing him in the flesh like that, without any warning or preparation, brought down all at once the doom of these swirling, storming thoughts.

Matty and I approached the common room and I tried to linger behind him—an effort to slip onto the scene unnoticed. But when I turned the corner, and the guys caught sight of me, Charlie shouted, "Hey, it's little Reensie!" and he laughed wildly. "What's up, girl? I haven't seen *you* in a bit."

"Hi." I waved timidly, feeling yellow and viscous.

Matty turned to me. "You two know each other?"

I gave a slight nod while Charlie called out, "Of course we do! Rinie, have a seat right here." He patted the space between himself and Andy.

"It's okay," I said. "I'll stand."

"Come on, now, don't be silly." This was Andy who spoke, with a smile so warm, so seemingly sincere, that I caught myself thinking, again, *He likes me,* before I told myself to cut it out.

"We won't bite," Andy added.

To sit or not to sit—a simple question, under ordinary circumstances. But nothing's been simple for me these days.

To sit, I could be expressing interest, reinforcing this man's image of me as compliant, willing, *easy;* I could be absolving him of any wrong-doing . . .

Which, I thought, might not be a bad thing.

Because to *not* sit was to *shun,* to express ill-will, to reinforce an unwillingness to fully forgive, or understand. By easing that,

I could act positively, compassionately, more *humanely*. Even if I am just a joke to them, it matters more to promote this more peaceful way of being, to demonstrate the value of doing so—and in doing so, make us all better.

Most importantly, though, which option would call the least attention to me? Which was the least obtrusive and potentially offensive? Which was the safest?

To sit, I decided, as I made my way over and sat. *You can do this,* I thought. *Just focus.*

"Spark it up!" Charlie cackled to Matty, who'd sat himself on the ottoman across from the couch. Matty obliged, and the joint-passing commenced.

When it came my turn, I gripped the delicate wrapping between two fingertips, curled my lips under, half-closed my eyes, and breathed in deep, deeper, then a little bit deeper than seemed possible. The room around me dissipated further into oblivion.

I don't think it was the pot, exactly, that made me feel changed, but more this taking in of breath—seeing the smoke, the physical proof of all I could hold. As I exhaled, I smiled—a real, unbounded smile, feeling entirely, in that moment, myself.

Sounds in the room melded into a single hum, thinly sliced by someone shouting, "Damn girl"—one of the guys. "Man, I've never seen a girl take a hit like that." In a wave of triumph, I felt large, and part of something larger, and higher; all the men in the room were tiny, indistinguishable, miles and miles below. *If only I could live like this forever,* I thought. I caught a glimpse of a possible future free of concern for such people and things. Time, as was the plan, did begin to slow, to the point where the space between each moment was so vast and magnified as to make all moments seem one.

This is freedom, I thought, and I tuned in to the jazz music blaring through the stereo speakers, closed my eyes and allowed my body to sway with each cadence, following the piano first, then the violin, the drums, the bass . . .

Then someone laughed sharply. Everyone's eyes were on me. "This song is so fucked up!" one of the guys said; I didn't know his name.

I listened more closely, to the words now, rather than just the rhythm. My cheeks went limp as all the muscles in my face gave way and I deciphered the words. The men's laughter intensified. "She sucked my . . ." "She licked my . . ." "Then I put my . . ."

What was this music, which sounded like jazz but veiled these words? Why would they play it? What were they trying to prove?

It was meanness, I decided. Just meanness, and I refused to participate.

I glared at each of them one by one and said, my heart beating fast, "Maybe we are what we hear," and then retreated again into the rhythm, tuning out the voices and any reaction or response. Even *I* didn't know what I meant by what I said, or if what I said was what I meant. I was all mixed up in meaning and wanted to move away from it. So I tried to transcend the moment, to tap into another, parallel one beyond that room and those people—I wanted to show them that it was possible, and necessary, to do so. Even for someone like me, and all that they seemed to think "someone like me" meant.

Minutes, hours—I couldn't tell how much time later, I heard Matty, a welcome voice, saying, "Okay, guys. I'm going to bed." I released a breath I'd been holding for what seemed like hours.

"Me too," I said, alert. "Night." I rose and waved casually, confidently, carelessly, and relished the experience of unconfused anger. And detachment.

Matty walked me to the door and stepped into the hall.

"Hey, sorry, those guys can be asses sometimes. Here." He handed me a joint from his pocket.

"I don't have any money on me."

"Just take it. You can buy me lunch next mall trip. Be careful walking home."

I smiled. "Thanks. Really," I said, and I left the building feeling vindicated and victorious. Freed from all the mess of feelings surrounding Andy. Done with it.

Later, restless, I rummaged for that joint, crept out into the common room, smoked it down, then crawled back into bed, where I stared at the television screen so long I started seeing things. The actors seemed to be calling my name, speaking directly to me, shouting, "Get out! Get out! Get out *now!*" The words and phrases taped on my walls seemed to throb and twist and morph—"Trust in heart," and "Nothing to Fear," became, "Trust Nothing," "Fear Heart." I thought of calling Steve—just to hear a familiar voice—but I resisted and somehow, some time, fell asleep.

And now, again, I am late for class.

The creative writing course is the only one I attend with anything resembling regularity. I haven't been to my Political Parties class in weeks—maybe even a month. I keep up with the syllabus, the readings, and the papers, and that, I believe, is enough. I can't bear to sit through it, surrounded by all those people, those wolves. That's how I feel—like a rabbit surrounded by salivating wolves.

As if I'm that important.

I dress quickly in sweatpants and a sweatshirt and reach the classroom only fifteen minutes late. For a two-and-a-half hour period, to me, that doesn't seem too bad. But I forget how often I've done this. As I enter the silent classroom, Professor

Snyder glances at me, then down at her papers, and says, "Rinie, please see me in the hallway. Class, continue your free-writing exercise."

I think I see smirks on my classmates' faces, but I can't be sure.

The door closes behind us and I begin my apologetic plea: "I'm so sorry. My alarm didn't go off. I set it wrong. Everything's just been so crazy for me lately, and . . ."

With arms folded across her chest, she says, "Irinie. This is unacceptable. You've been significantly late at least three times, and you've missed one entire class."

"I know," I say emphatically, "and I'm really sorry for that. But I've done all the work . . ."

She casts her long brown hair behind her shoulder, and I think about how she is so young, pretty . . . successful. How hard she must have worked to get here. How much effort it must take to maintain. How far I am from this type of composure. "Doing the work isn't enough," she says. "You need to be *here.*"

"But . . ."

"There's no point for you to stay today."

Professor's Snyder's voice is so even, so recitational, that I suddenly feel sorry for upsetting the balance of her world and her work. "You're going to fail if you don't drop the class."

Fail.

It's like sliding from a cliff, to hear the word. I've never failed a class, a paper, a test—anything. "But I've been working so hard on this project!" I try to steady my shaking hands and say, more calmly, "It's the only good thing I really care about right now." The truth of my own words is sobering, stunning. "I *need* to finish this."

She peers over my head. "I'm sorry, but there's simply no way you'll pass this course. I suggest you drop it, unless you want a D or an F on your transcript."

"I can't just quit!"

"You have no choice." She smiles and tips her head to the right. "Or, rather, you've made your choice." She glances down the hallway, left to right. Then her face and tone softens. "Listen, Rinie, it's just school."

Suddenly, I'm a four-foot-tall first-grader, and she's kneeling beside me, placing a bandage on a paper cut. *Just school?*

And with that, I slide further down the mountainside. School is my primary responsibility, the only thing that makes me feel even slightly human, whole, real; accountable, expected. Doing poorly in school makes me feel *less* human, whole, and real, but failing at it completely . . .

"But school is important," I manage.

"Yes, it is." Her words, now, are more breathy and nurturing. I can feel the sacrifice in this for her, to break form. "But life is *more* important."

It's a disorienting thought. "But I care about this class. It's the only one I can handle coming to at all . . ."

"But you know my policy." She dips her head to peek through the glass door pane. "Good luck, Irinie. I need to get back in there."

I watch her reenter the room, take her place at the front, and toss her hair back, before she begins speaking. Then I walk down the hall toward the exit. "You deserve this," I mutter. "You're such a fuck-up."

I hold the chapter, due today in a class that I no longer belong in, and tear it in half, then rip those halves in half, again and again, until I'm sure that no one could ever possibly paste those pieces together, even if someone for some otherworldly reason ever tried.

It's the Tuesday before Thanksgiving break, and though it's a big party night up at school, I decide to head home anyway. Rachel and some others are home, too, and a guy we know from high school—or, a guy Rachel knows, really—is having some people over.

My plan is to not get too drunk. To stay in control. I simply want to listen to some music, drink a drink, and try to stop thinking so much for a while.

So Rachel and another girl from high school, Sarah Mitchell, pick me up from my parents' house, and we head over to the party. When we get there, we grab drinks, and I stake out an isolated spot by a bookcase, to observe.

But there's something about a female standing alone at a party. Like a welcome mat.

Before long, a brown-haired guy named Tyler—the host—looking clean-cut and friendly in his blue-and-white-striped polo shirt and khaki-colored shorts, comes over and says, "I remember you."

I smile, because I've learned my lesson about being rude. "Tyler?"

"Right. And your name again?"

"Rinie."

He nods. "You were one year behind me at St. Mike's."

"Yep." I wait for him to say, "You were the one who dated Jack your freshman year," but he doesn't; he spares me.

"So you really like music, huh?"

The question befuddles me. "Yeah. Why do you ask?"

"Well, I see the way you're dancing over here by yourself, and . . ."

My cheeks burn, and I hang my head like a dog. "Was I?"

"You kinda were." His smile is sweet and warm, and I think, *Tyler is friendly. Very friendly.* But I won't allow myself to get carried away. "This is going to sound weird," I say, "but I

98

need you to understand that this is a totally platonic conversation."

He throws his head back in a laugh, revealing perfectly aligned white teeth. "Why would you say that?"

"It's nothing personal." I stir the ice cubes in my drink. "I just don't want to be sending off any vibes I don't mean to send."

"Don't worry, Rinie. You come off as totally platonic. No other vibes."

We talk for a while about music and learn that we like a lot of the same artists. I tell him about the playlist I've been listening to for the past month, and he tells me about the band he plays in. He offers to teach me guitar.

"You don't play an instrument?" he asks. I tell him no. "If you were to start playing an instrument right now, what would it be?"

I think for a moment, then say, decisively, "Piano."

His head bobs along with the beat of a funk song playing on the stereo. "I happen to have a piano upstairs. No time like the present."

I laugh and pull at a loose thread in my sweater. "I think it might take a little longer than that."

He shakes his head no. "Not really. You just gotta sit down and feel it."

Sit down and feel it. That seems like something I can do.

I look back at the crowded kitchen, where Rachel and Sarah are playing Beer Pong against two guys I've never seen before. There's a crowd around the table cheering them on. "I don't know . . ."

"C'mon, it'll be fun. Show me what you got."

His voice is soft and even, his eyes wide, his skin smooth and creamy, like a child's.

"All right," I say, "for a little while."

We climb the steps and he guides me toward a small room at the end of a hall, where the upright piano is against the back wall. Tyler ushers me over to the bench, says, "Take a seat," and sits beside me. When I look at him wearily, he says, "Relax. I just want to be up close to the music." I laugh a little and set my fingers on the keys, my thumb at middle C, as I learned from the *Teach Yourself to Keyboard* book my grandma bought me for Christmas when I was a kid. "Play," he continues. "Just close your eyes and feel it."

The room is quiet—no one else is on the second floor—so I do, I close my eyes and drill my fingers down, feeling my way through the sounds. I tap the keys as though I'm rapping fingernails on a desk, playing the same safe melody over and over, but with varying intensity, soft and light then strong and loud, then somewhere in between. The chords become an extension of all the tension stored within me. Not a thought in my mind, I barely hear the sound—I'm inside of it, feeling it, willing it, transferring pressure from within me into the keys. When there's nothing left, I place my hands on my lap and open my eyes. I stare at the artificial Easter lily plant on top of the piano; it seems to be laughing—at me or with me.

That's when Tyler places a hand on my right leg, his fingertips grazing just left of center. But the hand, to me, feels like it's reaching right inside me. My body jerks back, and a swell of anger rises into my throat. I push hard into his shoulders and he falls clumsily off the bench.

"What the hell?" he says from the beige carpeted floor.

I stand up from the bench and shake my head, then hold a hand out to help him up. "I'm sorry, Tyler. But I thought we agreed . . ."

He sits back down, facing me, and rattles his hands. "I know, I know. But I really like you. And I thought . . . "

"Tyler . . ."

"And we have so much in common."

"Oh, come on," I say with a laugh.

"*You* come on." He looks small, and hurt, and again I notice the butter-soft skin, the light, easy gaze.

"I'm sorry, Tyler. I honestly didn't mean to mislead you."

"Huh." He pinches his lips together and rocks a bit in his seat. "Hey, don't worry about it."

"I'm really sorry," I say, with a hand to my forehead. It's as if these words, *"I'm sorry,"* are the only ones I know anymore, the only feeling I can feel.

"It's fine. No worries. I gotta check on things." He gets up, walks past me and, without a glance in my direction, leaves the room.

On the car ride home, Sarah, who is in the passenger's seat, turns to face me. "So tell us how things went with *Tyler* up there," she says, with a grin.

My body stiffens. "We were just talking about music. I was playing his piano."

"Ha! That's a good one. 'Playing his piano.'" She winks at me.

The wink feels like a punch.

"I'm serious," I say, my voice flat and low. "We were just talking about music."

"Mm hm."

Even here, back home, they can smell it on me now.

I creep into the house. It's almost midnight, and everyone is asleep, including my father, who is on the couch with the television on—waiting for me, no doubt.

I fill a glass of water and take an apple from the fridge, sit down at the kitchen table, and slice the fruit slowly with a steak knife. My father releases an alarmingly loud snore, then sits up. He glances over his shoulder, sees me and says, "Baby girl. You're home."

I nod without looking up.

He stands and brushes his pajamas flat, then walks toward me. When he puts a hand on my shoulder, I push it away; he tries to give me a kiss on the cheek, but I jerk my face aside.

He pauses, then points to the fruit. "Just this you eat?"

I glower at him through my peripheral view. "It's all I want, an apple."

"Your mother made *pastitio.*"

I haven't eaten *pastitio,* a casserole of pasta, meat-sauce, and cream, in probably five years.

"No, thank you."

"It's so good. She makes the best, you know."

I nod, because I do know, but it doesn't make any difference. That food is beyond me.

Something comes to life in him, and he chops the air with his hands. In a voice more intense now, he says, "How can you live like this, on fruit, lettuce, broccoli?"

My insides percolate, but I try my best to stay calm and quiet. I've been through this with him too many times.

"You're like a spaghetti, so skinny," he continues.

The sound of that word *skinny* sets me off; like I'm weak, helpless, dumb. I punch a fist onto the table and glare at him. "I am *not skinny.* Leave me alone."

He lifts his hands in surprise. "What's the matter with you?"

I don't look up from my fruit. What is the *matter* with me?

Where would I even begin?

"What's going on with you, Irinie *mou*?" he persists. "Why are you so angry with me?"

I see the expression of hurt and concern on his grizzly face, but it means nothing to me in that moment. He's right, I *am* angry. Suddenly, I stand and scream: "I *am* angry! I *am!*"

He leans his head forward and cocks it to the right. "Why?"

"Why? Because you and mom and . . ." I want to say Mark, but I choke on his name, swallow hard, and continue. "You and mom taught me that men and women are the same, that women can do anything men can do. You told me that I could do anything, be anything, that it doesn't matter what anyone else thinks; that I can think for myself, that I was strong and tough, and you know what? You were *wrong!* I'm not strong, and that's not how the world works. The world is a fucked-up place."

I wipe saliva from my cheek and slump back down to my chair.

He looks serious, now, as if he's wondering which direction to take—to tell the little girl that she's right, that there is no Santa, or to chastise her for figuring it out too young. "*Irinie mou,*" he says.

"Don't worry about it," I tell him, and I stand. "It's not a big deal." I toss my half-eaten apple into the trash, pour out my water, and place my glass in the dishwasher. I stare him in the face. "Really, I'm fine." He is stunned as I brush past him and head to bed.

The next day, I am kind to him. We work together at the diner and fall back on our old routines—I work hard, he helps me out, we go home, and we have a nice big family dinner. I pretend to be my old self as best as I can.

But all of this takes something out of me.

Sunday night, back at school, I'm exhausted. I lay down in bed at 9 p.m. glad to be at rest, thankful that it won't be too hard to fall asleep, until a half hour later when my cell phone rings. I don't recognize the number and have an irrational thought that it must be something good, something hopeful. When I answer, it's a male voice on the other end: "Hi, is this Rinie?" I tell him that it is. "This is Andy," the voice continues.

The ceiling closes down on me, the walls press in. I try to sound casual, friendly. "Oh, hi!"

"Hi." He takes a second. "Listen, it seems to me that you've been talking some shit."

The room spins, and my breathing shallows. "What?"

"You've been spreading some rumors about me."

Is this real? "What do you mean?"

"At the bar last week before break, some random girl came up to me, all wasted, and accused me of . . ." He sighed. "Some terrible things."

"I . . . I don't know who would have done that."

And I don't. My memory, of late, has been operating like a fish's, in short bursts.

After a pause, he says, "Do you know who I am?"

He says it the first time with the sound of genuine inquiry. The second time, he adds more emphasis—"Do you *know* who I *am*?"—as though he is speaking to two different people: one innocent, one not.

No I don't, I want to say. *And I don't* want *to know.* But my throat constricts, as if it were encased with wet asphalt.

"You can't go around saying shit like that, if you don't know who you're dealing with. And I don't think you know who I am . . ."

"Please," I whisper. "Relax. I . . . it must be a misunderstanding. We talked about this."

"Right," he says, a tad calmer. "That's what I thought."

104

"No, we did. I can't imagine who would have said that . . ." It hits me at once. *Kathryn, you idiot. Who else?* "We . . . we have an understanding. We talked about this."

"Right. Yes. But sometimes, girls, you know . . . they say that, but then . . . Well, okay. I'm just saying . . ."

"No, no, I know." I'm nodding so hard as if he can see me; as if that can make this stop. "I'm not looking to get anyone in trouble . . ."

Again, I shake my head *no*.

There's a pause, and then he sighs again. "Okay. So we're good?"

"Yes, yes, we're good. Good."

I let the phone drop to the bed and think, *Water.*

I walk out to the kitchen, where Kathryn is sitting on a stool at the counter. "Rinie," she says. "You okay? You're white as a ghost."

"You . . ." Her face is blurred, and I fight to bring it into focus. "I . . . just . . . need water." She fetches me a filled glass, and I down it all at once. I stare at the ceiling, because I can't bear to see her face, calm and fine, at the same time I'm coming apart. I shout, "You *told* him! You fucking *told* him!"

She runs her fingers through her hair. "What do you mean? Told who what?"

"Him! You know!" I'm out of breath and words.

Her head jerks back and she blinks dramatically. "Are you talking about Andy? Because if you're talking about Andy. . ."

"Do not. Do not say that name to me, ever!" I scream, before collecting myself to say, "Please, Kathryn, I'm sorry, but I don't ever want to talk about this with you again."

She shrugs and shakes her head. "Have it your way."

I head off to my bed, turn on the television, and fall into a rock hard sleep.

Around 1 a.m., I wake to darkness, save for the television's glow.

"A rotten person," I hear someone say. "Rotten to the core."

That's right, I think. *I am.* I press the "off" button on the remote control, but the silence reveals a strange hum. The sound of nothing.

I flick back on the television and flip through the channels. *"A small plane crash killed four people in southern New Hampshire late last night . . . "* I quickly switch the station again, mute the volume, and turn the music on my computer to the lowest level of sound. My left arm feels heavy, deadened as if shot with lead bullets.

I'm having a heart attack.

My jaw aches, and I rub a soreness below my ear. A lump?

The Neil Young song "Everybody Knows This Is Nowhere" plays softly, eerily, through the darkness, and I think, *It is. It is nowhere.*

I reach for my cell phone. Who can I call? My parents and sisters must be sleeping. Steve?

I am alone, I think. *I have always been alone. All these people have been illusions. And now that I know, now that I've figured it all out, they're gone.*

I put the phone back on my desk.

Am I even alive anymore?

I pick up the phone again, dial Steve's number, and press send, but I end the call before the first ring.

My left arm feels too heavy to move now as the right one tightens, too. Will each of my limbs begin to die this slow death, one by one?

Maybe I'm dreaming. Maybe I'm stuck in between . . .

That's when I hear Kathryn's soft snoring—a sign of life. I tiptoe to her side of the room and touch her shoulder. Her eyes slit open as she says, "Rinie. What's wrong?"

"I"—my mouth is dry and lined with cotton—"can't sleep. I . . . am really scared."

"What are you scared about?"

I shake my head. "Is this real?"

"Rinie, what are you talking about?"

"Can you just tell me if this is real?"

"If what is real?"

"This! This room, this pencil holder." The pencils rattle as I lift the object from her desk and set it down. I point to the television. "That." I wave my arm toward the window. "This school, this place. This world. Just tell me if it's real or if it's just in my head."

"Listen," she says, eyes closed, head at rest on the pillow, "everything is fine. You just need some sleep."

"I can't. Can't sleep. I'm too scared . . ."

"You have to try . . ."

"Do you think I'm a horrible person? Like, a secretly evil person, and I don't even know it?" I hover above her, like a ghoul.

She turns her head to the side and says into the pillow, "Rinie. You. Are. Not. A. Horrible. Person," enunciating each word. "You're a nice person. You're just overly exhausted and need to get to bed."

I look at the space beside Kathryn. "Can I stay here on your side of the room? I don't want to be alone right now."

She inches toward the wall. "Sure. Lie down and go to sleep."

"Thank you," I breathe. "You won't even notice me." I lie down, as close to the edge as possible to ensure that not one speck of my body imposes on hers.

Soon, I fall asleep.

CHAPTER EIGHT
AGE NINETEEN

I met Steve during the fall of my sophomore year of college, at a party I went to with Rachel, with whom I'd rekindled a tepid friendship over instant messenger while she was down at school in Delaware, and I up in Boston.

It was Thanksgiving break, and the party was at our high school classmate Phil's house. I was nervous about going, because I hadn't spoken with these people in a couple of years, but we got there late, thankfully, so most of the guests were sufficiently inebriated by the time we arrived. We were able to slink onto the scene largely unnoticed. I waved from afar to most of my old friends and acquaintances, spoke briefly to a few, and there were enough new faces—mostly Phil's friends from the local state college he attended—to make the whole event not so bad.

One of those new faces was Steve's.

As Rachel and I poured ourselves some boxed wine in the kitchen, Phil swept in and said, "Girls, let me introduce you to my friend here."

The most distinctive thing about Steve was that he wore a rounded fisherman's hat the color of peat moss, with a powder-blue feather shooting up from the side. His sandy brown hair curled up in waves around his ears. His green eyes were soft in tone, almost gray, and when Phil announced his name, Steve smiled, cocked his head to the right, glanced upward, and declared, "Yep, that's me!"

We all said our hellos. I put my hand out to shake Steve's,

and he immediately said, "Oh, I like your bracelet." I looked down at my wrist, at the braided net of yellow and green yarn wrapped around it.

"Um, thanks," I said. I'd put it on a month before and forgotten it. "My nephew made it for me at his nursery school."

"Your nephew made it for you at his nursery school," he parroted, smiling and still shaking my hand. "That's so adorable."

"Thanks," I said, my hand limp. "It's true, he's adorable."

"Rinie, let's go say hi to Sarah and Mark," Rachel said, rescuing me from having to chat with this odd one in the hat. And so we waved goodbye and made a brief round about the room before I hunkered down alone by the fireplace in a well-worn armchair.

Before long, Steve found me there. Standing above me, he said—as if continuing an existing conversation, "So."

I released a small laugh. "So."

He placed a pointer finger to his mouth. "I feel like I've met you before. Have we met?"

I peered at him through squinted eyes. "Mmm, I don't think so."

He tapped a foot, then shrugged. "Maybe you're just one of those people."

"One of what people?"

"You know. Those people with faces you feel like you've seen before. What is up with that?"

"What do you mean?" I said, though I knew exactly what he meant. In truth, I had wondered about this myself. Many times. Sometimes to the point of dwelling on it. But offering that kind of revelation seemed like trouble; I'd be inviting an intimacy of thoughts I wasn't prepared for.

"It's not like you have a common face or anything," he continued. "I mean, there can't be more than one of a face like yours."

"What?" I wasn't sure how to take this and wished, at once, that I wore a mask.

"Well, it's very unique."

"Um . . ."

He threw his head back in a chuckle. "It just is, it's different. You've got all these cute, rounded features, and when you smile you look . . ."

"Please." *Cute, rounded features.* "I don't need to hear any more."

He took a seat on the brick step in front of the fireplace. "Why not?"

I averted my eyes and said nothing. Without intending to, I'd drawn him closer, and now I needed to shirk him off.

"You're a very interesting-looking person," he said, in case I hadn't gotten his message yet.

"Please," I repeated.

"I mean that in a good way."

"*Please,*" I pleaded.

"What?"

"Don't."

I asked about the hat. He explained it was a gift from his father, who'd received it as a gift from *his* father. "We're Minnesota men," he said, as if that explained everything. "I come from a long line of fishermen."

"So you like to fish?"

He chuckled again, an almost giggle. "No. I actually hate to fish. Only because I can't swim."

"You can't swim?"

"Nope," he said, punctuating the "p" and lifting his chin as though proud of this fact. "I'm deathly afraid of water."

I felt suddenly and starkly unsettled, as if, by mention of water, the room had become a ship, and we'd been set adrift at sea. I looked at Steve and wondered if he had been right after all, if we had met before, in some time I could no longer recall.

"I'm scared of fish, too," he said, and when he laughed, I couldn't help but laugh as well.

That's when Rachel came by and asked if I was ready to go. I slapped my hands onto my thighs and said, "Yes, actually I am. I've got to work early in the morning anyway."

"Work?" he said. "On Thanksgiving?"

"I work at my father's diner," I explained. "We're open on Thanksgiving."

He smiled and began his parroting act again: "You work with your father, on Thanksgiving."

"I do." I stood and added in a tone that aimed to be at once polite and conclusive, "It's like a tradition now."

He laughed that laugh again with his head tilted back and to the left. I felt compelled to say, "What's so funny?" but it didn't seem worth the trouble.

"What's the name of the diner?" he asked.

I glanced at Rachel, who offered no expression. "City Square," I said.

He nodded. "Take care, then, Rinie. Maybe I'll see you soon."

At 8:00 a.m. the next morning, he showed up at the diner, with a man he introduced as his father. The two were headed to the high school football game in their town, Steve explained, but both had a craving for some hearty eggs Benedict before-hand.

From a diner that happened to be 25 minutes away.

I spotted him in the corner of my eye from where I stood taking down an order; he was in the doorway, scanning left to right. While I said, "White, wheat, or rye toast?" to my bonneted, church-going regular, Millie, I saw my father walk up to Steve and his dad and ask his usual question: "How many?" The expression on my father's face shifted from a standard taking-care-of-business look to one of confusion while he spoke to this young man, who pointed in my direction.

From Millie and her husband Lester's table, I took a circuitous route into the kitchen, where my father met me. "They ask for your section," he said, reading my mind. "The young one say he knows you."

I nodded as I piled bacon onto a plate of scrambled eggs. "Yeah, I know him."

He fiddled with a bucket of butter chips. "Oh. Okay." After a long pause, he added, "He seem nice."

"Eh," I shrugged. "I need a side of home fries!" I called to the cooks.

My father ducked under the plate warmer that separated us from the grillmen. "Guys, easy on the potatoes, huh? Not so much on the plate."

With the armor of my waitressing uniform and duties, it was easy to remain both warmly polite and distanced from Steve and his father who, like his son, seemed instantly comfortable chatting it up with me. "Your father," the dad—who I later knew as Stan—said. "What a great guy. Where's he from?" I told him where, and Stan was ecstatic. "An island man, like me!" Stan had spent his summers, he said, in a little bungalow on an island in Minnesota's Lake Vermillion. "But Greece. Boy. What history! And those Greeks. Such hard workers. I mean, look at this place." He waved his arms dramatically, indicating the span of the diner. "I respect that."

So glad, I wanted to say dryly, but I smiled as I would at any customer and said, "Yes, he's worked hard."

That night, after my shift and an elaborate family dinner, during which I left my cell phone in my bedroom, I saw that I had a voicemail. "Hey!" said an exuberant voice. It was Steve's. "I hope you didn't work too hard today. It was nice to see you, and I hope you had a great Thanksgiving. I'm having some people over tomorrow—Phil, some others. And I'd love it if you came. Also, I'd just like to talk to you on the phone." He left his number and asked me to call him back that night, any time.

How had he gotten my number? Presumably from Phil, who got it from Rachel.

What was all this attention? Why to me?

I'd begun, lately, to wonder if a guy would ever be interested in me again. I'd taken to thinking of myself as someone who was meant to be alone—someone who would someday, if things worked out, have a sprawling property in, say, the Florida Keys, with a funky little tin-roofed cottage, surrounded by orchids and hibiscus, with orange and lemon and lime trees sprouting up and growing out around me. I'd live and work there as an artist of some kind—a writer, maybe, or a painter—and I'd teach classes to people who wanted to "find themselves" through their art. My married, busy, bustling friends and relatives from the cities and suburbs would fly down for respites, and I'd set out lawn chairs, serve them freshly-squeezed orange juice and slices of homegrown mango, and I'd invite them to relax, to visit a life they would never, themselves, desire full time but would need, every once in a while, to remember themselves, and why. They'd return to their lives *better,* and that would be my contribution to the world.

But despite this rapturous dream, my ego was still kicking about beneath the tarp under which I'd buried it, and this attention from Steve felt pretty good.

So, to call back or not. The question twisted me up for an hour. On one hand, it would be rude—hurtful, even—not to call back. On the other hand, it could be misleading to do so; it could be perceived as a sign of interest, and is that really what I wanted to deliver?

But why make such an ordeal out of something so small? *Someone calls you*, I thought, *you call them back*.

So I did.

Steve called me every night for the next month, and we chatted on the phone for hours. It was a pleasant distraction at first, and eventually something to look forward to at the end of a long and lonely school day. We talked mostly about the ordinary details. Sometimes we didn't talk at all—we stayed on the phone watching the same sitcoms at the same time and reacting as though we were in the same room.

I came home a couple times during that period, to waitress at the diner, and he invited me to his house to hang out. The first time, Phil was there, too, and the three of us sat in Steve's basement watching the movie *Spaceballs*. They couldn't believe I didn't find the film funny, or that I had to turn away from the scene where the singing alien bursts through the guy's stomach. "Come on, lighten up!" Steve said, wrapping an arm around my waist. The old blue couch with the squeaky springs left me little support, so when my body lurched toward him, it felt good and warm, so I left it there, pressed against him, throughout the remainder of the movie.

Phil was barely up the stairs after calling it a night when Steve kissed me for the first time, and after that hour or so with the side of my body touching his, I was ready for it. I kissed him, too, and felt his warm hand on my back, first above, then

114

below my sweater, on my bare, cool skin, grazing the bones of my spine with his fingers.

"You're so skinny," he said, and I shrunk back, glancing down at the faded-blue tweed-patterned fabric of the couch. "I mean, it's fine. It's just that I didn't realize."

We kept on kissing. Then he cradled my back to lay me down flat. It was far beyond my usual range of comfort. And yet with Steve, it was possible. In a way, this physical way, he took things slow and easy. All those weeks on the phone, I felt I knew him, like he was just a really good friend that I could now kiss and cuddle with.

This cuddling became my favorite part about nights with Steve. His warm hands on my body, his fingers pressed into the slope of my lower back; the palm of his hand resting on my chest bones. My leg squished tight between his thighs, my toes curled under his calves, my head on his collarbone, his lips on my hair.

I agreed to be his girlfriend in a complicated combination of not wanting, or not knowing how, to say no. I liked talking to him on the phone; I liked our nights in his basement. But I had never trusted any interest males seemed to take in me—I perceived it as misguided, guided by some false or incredibly partial notion of who I was: the nice little Greek girl; the smart girl who likes to read; the quiet, moody one too cool for school. Who knows what they saw. And Steve was no exception.

But he *insisted*—in fact, he "wouldn't take no for an answer," he said, even as I repeatedly explained my determination to ultimately remain alone in life. That's how badly he wanted to be with me, how much he liked me, I reasoned, and so how could I let him down? How could I outright reject someone so openly expressing a desire, a near *need*, to be with me?

Also, it was flattering. He told me I was beautiful, and even though I didn't believe it—I believed he wore the rosiest shade of rose-colored lenses possible when it came to me—it was nice to rest for a while in that comfort. His unwillingness to relent made me believe that maybe, just maybe, whatever he saw in me was not, in fact, an illusion, but some real, actual goodness, a goodness that might even be sustainable.

There was the fact, too, that I liked him. He was kind and sensitive and quirky; he seemed to need me, and I liked to be needed.

But the problem I sensed was that he wanted me to need him just as much. And for years, I'd been actively trying to free myself from need as much as possible, to confine my sense of it to the actual essentials—food, water, clothing, shelter, air.

So I set my boundaries. Even as I became his girlfriend, I wouldn't allow him to talk about a "future" together; I let him know that, in the end, my plan was still to be alone.

But there was another convenience in being with Steve. He helped me feel *normal.*

Before meeting Steve, the only boy I'd kissed was a kid named Bill Brennan at a party in my sophomore year of high school; we were both tipsy off the purple wine coolers some other kid brought along, and we caught ourselves laughing too wildly at the same joke. He leaned in to kiss me and I let him, and we made out for ten minutes sitting upright on the carpeted floor, each of us with a shoulder against a wall.

So after four and a half months as Steve's girlfriend, I agreed to sleep with him. I was nineteen years old, and it seemed like the time to do so. He was thrilled, and I could tell he enjoyed being the more experienced one, showing me everything, every step of the way, in a voice over, as if he were starring in a how-to video about the proper way to build a deck.

After that first night, I laid on the bed in my pink-walled bedroom, my down floral comforter pulled to my chin, and gazed around the room my mom had decorated for me in high school, made to look more grown up and mature—the wrought-iron bedposts at the foot and behind my head, in the shape almost of a flame; the burgundy drapes with their lustrous sheen and ruffled valance; the yellow bureau that had been handed down to me from Eugenia, who'd gotten it from Vicky, and which I'd had in my room since age eleven; beside it, a tall vase with artificial snapdragons, white and lavender, bounding upward from the base. I'd never grown into this room, and even now, it still didn't seem like I was old or mature or "real" enough for it. Sex didn't make me feel as different as I imagined it would. A man, or a part of a man, had entered my body. It was a man I cared about and trusted—but what had changed? Why didn't it seem to mean all that everyone said it should?

If anything, it made me more potently aware of an emptiness inside me, like something was lost and gone. Wasn't I supposed to feel something heavier? Guilt, at least? Everything I'd ever learned about sex had been from Catholic school; neither one of my parents had ever spoken the word in my presence. So wasn't this step *supposed* to come with guilt, especially when you knew deep down that this wasn't the person you were meant to be with forever? When you *knew* this person wasn't "the one"? When you believed, in fact, that there *was* no "one" for you?

But instead, as time passed, I felt relief. No matter how badly a day might go, in the back of my mind, I took comfort in knowing that I'd checked off a milestone. It—*sex*—was no longer a thing to worry about. In those who knew what it was all about, I no longer sensed a superiority; I no longer felt inadequate for not knowing about the mystery. And what mystery? It was nothing but physical sensation. All that hype, it seemed, for very little.

Steve and I went to the movies once, to see *The Lord of the Rings,* a film I didn't understand at all, but I liked the colors and scenery, and that was enough. Afterward, we went to Denny's—Steve's favorite—and he ordered a chicken pot pie, a thing I'd never seen anyone but my grandmother eat, and even she only ate it once at a strange little restaurant in a shopping plaza we came upon during a road trip through Pennsylvania.

That trip to Denny's with Steve was our only real date, and it was about three months into our six-month relationship. The rest consisted of phone conversations and cuddling in his basement after dark.

But sometimes, when I looked at Steve—no matter how intensely—I got the sense that I couldn't see him at all. And I knew he couldn't see me, either. I knew he felt the need to protect me from something, and there were times I wondered if he was right; if he'd been set on my path for a reason—to save me from an unknown danger.

I didn't want that to be true, so I willed it away. I needed to escape him.

But every time I left him on a Saturday night, and drove back up to Boston, and thought about breaking up with him, I thought about that goddamn chicken pot pie—how adorable and sad it was at the same time. I thought about his Sega Genesis remote controls tangled in front of the couch where he spent half his life in those days; that fisherman's hat he wore to the party, even though he was afraid of the water, and fish. How could I hurt such a person, who was so soft and raw, like the skin beneath a peeled-away scab?

This, all along, had been the real danger—that I'd be drawn so closely to another human being that it would feel impossible to let go.

One cloudy Saturday morning in late spring, in his parents'

driveway, I broke up with Steve. We'd had plans to go straw-berry picking, but I explained that I couldn't go; I couldn't con-tinue the relationship, in fact—I just needed to be alone. It wasn't him, of course, it had always been me, I assured him; I should never have allowed either of us to get involved, and he was better off without me.

"I don't accept it," he said with a smile. "I don't need your protection, and I know this isn't over."

I looked down at the damp pavement and shook my head. "No sad goodbyes, okay? I don't believe in them."

He smiled and poked me in the stomach. "You're such a tough girl."

"I am," I said, without a smile. "Good luck with every-thing."

I hugged him, climbed back into the car, and was surprised to find myself unable to peek into the rearview mirror as I drove away; unable, in fact, to drive beyond a half mile down the road before pulling over and bursting into tears.

Which is exactly how I knew the right decision had been made.

CHAPTER NINE
EARLY MAY

I am going to die soon.

Or, someone I love, too much . . . someone I can't live without, like my mom, my dad—I won't even think of my sisters—is going to die soon. Someone whose life is so intrinsically linked to my own as to create, through its termination, an abscess within me, one that will gradually spread at a rate of speed I won't be able to foresee.

This is the message the universe has been trying to send me. This is the imminent disaster I've been trying to prepare for, for years.

Because of this—because I am *aware* of this—there's not much else that can affect me. It puts everything into perspective. I'm at the mercy and service of the world, let it do with me what it will.

By now, near the end of the school year, my avoidance of class has increased to an almost comical degree; it's less of a daily and more like a monthly consideration. Mostly I show up on days with tests, which can't be made up afterward, but for every other assignment, I simply read the books and write the papers in coffee shops or in my favorite nook on the top floor of the library, or in the middle of the night, in the darkness of my dorm room lit by nothing but the beam of my computer screen. To teachers who allow it, I email the work; to the others, I slip the papers under their office doors—an act of good faith, a hope that they will earnestly accept it. But even if they don't, it doesn't matter. Doing the work matters, because *some-thing* has to matter, but whether or not it "counts" is not that thing.

Class is not that thing. It is equally disheartening to find a bored professor dictating a tired speech as it is to see an impassioned one interrupted by comments like, "Will this be on the test? And if so, can you repeat that more slowly?" *Fuck* that is what I think.

Today, though, I've got a test in my Politics of Eastern Europe class, so I've got to go.

Which is tough, because I woke today with an achy back and throat, and an exacerbated case of my perpetual fatigue.

It's the weather, I assume. I am sledging through muddy wet grass up the hill on my way to the street where I park my car, and the rain is pouring down hard. It is after 9 a.m., so it doesn't surprise me that I can see, from fifty feet away, a bright orange parking ticket on my windshield. I've been parking in this same spot all year, essentially a free spot between 6 p.m. and 9 a.m., but I rarely wake up early enough anymore to move the car in time.

I lean over the windshield to grab the ticket, but it's so moistened from the rain that it splits like a slice of melted cheese as I pull. *Let it crust up,* I decide, *and I'll grab it tomorrow, with the new one.* Or better yet . . .

I fire up the engine, drive out of my spot, and flick on the wipers, flinging the notice off into oblivion.

I have no idea what's on the test today—a final, actually— but I've read all the books on the syllabus: *The Communist Manifesto, The Balkan Ghosts, The Walls Come Tumbling Down.* I read in the way a woman on a mission might—intensely, with fervor, as if there is a code to crack, on an urgent quest, with a sense that something is following behind me, and with a dire need to get to that place of discovery before that "something else" does. My gaze remains set acutely in the direction of my target destination—the gut of truth. No time for stopping on such a journey to browse through the souvenirs of detail—in which year did this happen, in what city that? Which rich white man did this, and which one did that? In everything I read and do and think, these days, I have one question. Actually, two: what does it all mean—and does it mean anything at all?

So I'm fairly certain I will flunk the test, but showing up, I know, counts for something.

What I don't know is answers to multiple choice questions like, "Which of the following was *not* an agreement of the Warsaw Pact?" and "In what year did the Soviets launch Sputnik?" Doesn't ring a so-called bell. Important facts, but only for people with the luxury of time and finer responsibility, greater expectations, higher and more concrete, life-based callings. My plan is to simply focus on the essay, because you can always get some points on the essay, especially with questions as broad as this one: "What caused the communist system in Eastern Europe to collapse?"

The enormity of the question, paired with the virtual impossibility of anyone knowing such an answer definitively, let alone a college undergrad who spent a couple months reading some books, makes me smile; makes me feel a kind of *tharos*— freedom, courage—and an ease I experience rarely these days, only in those quiet moments when I look straight at a thing and know, without a doubt, that I see it for what it is: in this case, an absolute paradox. A demand for an answer where no answer can exist.

I've always had this latent suspicion of a secret out there that everyone in the universe knows except me. A feeling that either the entire world is crazy or that I am, but it's one way or the other. That feeling's been compounded lately, while my interpretation of which answer is most accurate swings furiously between the two poles: *I am crazy*, which is what I most often believe: *I know nothing and am lost. I can't see what others see, can't hear what they hear, can't know what they know. There is nothing I can trust; certainly not my own sense.*

But every once in a while, I get this surge of—I don't know what to call it, hope? Faith? Belief? Insanity?—and then I think, no, *no*, the rest of the world is crazy, I see something they can't, and that thing is the true nature of the universe . . . or lack thereof.

In more rational moments, I think that maybe the whole world isn't crazy, but much too much of it is. Much too much of it operates on a shared assumption, a false acceptance of this farce we call "reality." The surface of things, of being, of the world and human bodies—all of it is an allusion that the mass of us believes in, every moment of every day, without question. Because questioning that notion is *terrifying*. Simple and obvious, but *terrifying*. I know because I've peeked behind that flimsy curtain, looked into the face of the Gorgon.

That's a word I learned in my Ancient World Literature class—the Gorgon is the one of three sisters you don't want to look directly at and truly see. Yeah, I know what that means.

My classmates, no doubt, are scribbling furiously now, spouting out "without a doubts" and "it is clear thats." But what could be so clear, so certain, without a doubt? Nothing. That, I know. And so in this rare moment of certainty—because the only thing you can be certain of in life is the truth of that very uncertainty—I write:

> *People seem to say the same thing about communism: a great idea on paper, in theory, in a perfect world—an ideal. Not so great in reality.*

> *True, of course, true. But isn't that a bit too simple, too quick, too easy? To place all the blame on theory and ideals, on paper and the impossibility of a perfect world? When do we start to look at humans, ourselves, as the problem? We are the problem. Communism is a good idea. Ideas are good. It is we who are bad.*
>
> *Not always, but just enough. And just when we least expect it. Therein lies the problem, maybe. Because we're good often enough for us to believe that we are always good, or more good than not, or good enough to do something good sustainably.*
>
> *But people, too often, are bad. We can't help it. Or, we can. But we don't. We don't fight our innate badness the way we should. Or could. Or would need to, for something like communism to work.*

I take a break and figure I should throw in some terms from the class.

> *Glasnost. Perestroika. Two more good ideas that were supposed to help but just made everything worse in the end. Of course!*
>
> *Let's start with* glasnost. *Openness. Ha! Imagine! Human openness being a good thing. Well it is, of course. It is a good thing—again, in theory. The problem is, one person says, "Let's be open." The other person says, "Okay, yeah, let's be open. One, two, three, go!" Wink, wink. One becomes open, while the other pretends to be, but actually closes a glass door. Or a two-way mirror. Behind which he can laugh, and* take.
>
> *This* taking *is the problem. Taking doesn't fit well into a true sense of communion. You don't* take *communion in the church, you* partake *of it, when it is offered to you as a gift—which you, in turn, must revere.*

I glance up at my professor—a middle-aged man with stringy blonde hair to his shoulders, wearing a rumpled, light-gray suit—who is gazing in my direction. I imagine myself appearing wild-eyed and disheveled, and I regret that, but it doesn't matter; I'm onto something. I take a deep breath and continue:

> And perestroika. "Restructuring." Change. What that requires to work is also impossible. It also demands a total buy-in that is not truly achievable, even when there is, ostensibly, unanimous agreement. "Sure, yeah, let's change things. Let's take that plunge. Let's be different." But then half the people jump off the cliff, and the other half stays behind. And then those people who stayed behind rule things, while the others splat to the ground.
>
> And there you have it: Power. People, more than anything, want to have power over one another.

I lift my pencil and release a small laugh. I laugh at everything—myself, the person I've been the last few months, years, my whole life—and it's a relief to be able to do so. I shake my head with shut eyes, then return to writing:

> Fear is the easiest way to keep people in power, in more ways than one. Powerful people are afraid. Those people leaping off cliffs, flying in the face of fear, relinquishing all need for power— they may be fearless, but they are fools. Fools for believing that the others would jump along with them. That doesn't make them—the fools—bad, but it *does* give those who didn't *jump* a reason to feel okay about themselves: "They should have known better," they think. "They are fools. Fools

don't deserve power. So we take it."
And there's that taking again. "They want us to
take it."
I'm sorry, but fuck those people. They are
wrong. About that, at least, but they are right about
one thing: trusting all of humanity to jump with you
at the same time is foolish. Believing it will happen
is perilous. Someone is playing chicken while
you're busy being "glasnost."

And, period. I flick my pencil down and exhale loudly,
which draws another look from the teacher. I place my head on
the desk until he announces that the test is over and that it's
time to turn in our blue books.

After class, I buy a banana from the coffee bar in the student union, then flop onto the grass in the courtyard, where I
lie on my back and pick tiny pieces off to nibble bit by bit.

All those thoughts swirling out like that on the test—it felt
draining, both inflating and deflating. These subjects, of goodness and badness, have been on my mind for a while, though
my attitudes toward them shift and mutate constantly, like tra-
peze artists contorting themselves around a horizontal bar before flinging themselves off to another and then back. The lead
performer of late has been the one who wants to combat this
badness, this innate sinfulness. It appears now that another,
new performer is emerging as the star.

My mother has always told me, "Don't ever judge other
people. You don't know what they deal with, who they are, and
what they feel in their hearts, no matter what they do and say.
Pay attention to yourself, to what you do and say. That's all that
matters." She was right, of course, but I never knew just *how*
right until this school year, which has prompted a deep and

probing inquiry into my own character, and what I've uncov-
ered by scraping off the surface is not what I wanted to see. As
hard as I've always worked to be good, I am still so far from
being as good as I want to be. I still have negative thoughts
about others. I still get jealous and wish I were as pretty or as
lucky or as loved as others. And I know that, while people like
Agnes and Sarah Mitchell may whisper and spread rumors
about me behind my back, I am not innocent of gossiping—
I've spent time with my cousins and sisters analyzing people
and saying things that are less than nice. And how about those
years I spent toying with my family's emotions while I starved
myself for my own personal pleasure? How about the fact that
I thought of Daniella and Jasmine in the beginning as my "first
black friends," instead of as just really great people?

How about letting Mark walk out that door unforgiven?
How about that?

You need to be careful about these things, about what you
say and think and even see. It can cause real harm in the world.
You can hurt a person with the evil eye—you can hurt, or even
kill, them.

But I've been trying not to dwell so much on this badness
lately, not even on my own—although that's harder to ignore. I
tell myself, *This badness does not make you special; you are not unique;
we all have this.* Because the point is to work to move beyond it,
even if doing so isn't fully possible. The point is to *try*, to wage
a nonviolent war of sorts.

That is what Jesus would do, and even though religion itself
is one big Gordian knot of confusion for me lately, I do know
that living as they say—or as my Intro. to Christian Theology
professor says—Jesus lived can't hurt and makes sense to my
mind. "Love your enemies," Jesus said—"Bless them that curse
you, do good to them that hate you, and pray for them which
spitefully use you, and persecute you."

127

Persecute you. That's Agnes. Here's a little example: Late one night, I was up watching TV in the common room on our floor. The room has two parts, divided by a kitchen, and Agnes and some friends of hers were hanging out on the opposite side. Apparently they didn't know I was there, because a guy who I've seen before and know is named Mikey said to Agnes, "So what's up with that girl Rinie? She's cute. Seems nice, too. I don't know why you hate her so much."

Agnes replied, "She's a dumb bitch."

A train-derailing moment. I wanted to stop listening, to stand up and show my face and bring the conversation to a halt, but I felt gripped by a dark, paralyzing desire to hear what would come next.

"You're crazy," Mikey said. "That girl is a . . . a sweet little bunny rabbit."

"Sweet little bunny rabbit my ass."

"Ah, you're too hard on her."

"Seriously, I'm not. And if you go near her I'll never speak to you again."

At least then I knew for sure what I'd suspected: she hated me and considered me an enemy. And you know what? I wasn't so thrilled about her either. But I understood why she didn't like me. We were so different. And I made a big mistake. I let her walk home alone. Now that I knew for sure that she hated me, it was material I could handle. So I wrote her a letter.

It said,

> *I know that you hate me. I know that you don't want your friends near me. And I understand. I just want you to know that I think deep down you are a nice person—I've seen the pictures of you hugging your little nieces, the framed photo of your dog, the way you drive the girls around and let them share your stash of diet soda and pita chips. I know I'm not perfect. Far from it. I'm sorry*

if I have offended you. I'm sorry for that night I let you
walk home alone. I do wish we could be friends, but I
know that may not be possible. I do wish for peace,
though, between us.

After that, I saw her out one night in a loud and crowded bar, and she bought me a drink. Came right up to me, with her arm linked in Mikey's, and handed me a tall glass of vodka Sprite. She put a hand on his back and mine and gave us a sideways hug, then shuffled away toward her friends. Mikey and I smiled awkwardly at one another and talked for a minute or two before politely retreating in our respective directions.

Agnes and I aren't exactly friends now, but we do say *hi* and smile at each other in the hall.

"Whoever slaps you on your right cheek, turn to him the other also," Jesus says. "If someone takes your cloak, do not stop him from taking your tunic." Cloaks and tunics aside, it's a great way of thinking, really. If hate has nothing to receive it—if I make myself an unreceptive agent—well then, that hate will break down, dissipate, and eventually cease to exist.

But now I've starting to see that if that's true of hate, then it's likely true of love, too.

If you live your life this way, with a commitment to giving freely, of all that you have, for the greater good—if you choose to surpass all negativity and bitterness, all anger and hate, and live your life essentially for the betterment of others—you're inevitably seen as strange, bizarre.

I went home last weekend, to meet up with some friends I had reconnected with on instant messenger. I'm in the habit of that these days. As I lie awake in bed at night, my mind scrolls through reels of footage within my short- and long-term memory, until the face of someone in particular comes into clear view, someone who may be hurting in a way I failed to see before, in all those years I spent thinking only of myself, of my own needs and fears. I think of people I didn't even know very well, like Larry Connor, who started acting strange sophomore year of high school, shouting out random phrases during history class. He went away to some hospital for two weeks and came back to incessant teasing from all his baseball teammates. "Larry the Loon" is what they called him. He just smiled and laughed, because what else could he do?

So when I think of a person like Larry, I do not just pray and think about, but actively try to imagine and experience his suffering. It's a way of putting to use this ability I've always had, but haven't been utilizing in the last few years; an extrasensory capacity to feel what others feel—in essence, to feel *for* them: to see in an instant, through intense concentration, into the nature of their suffering, and thereby absorb and diminish it.

I apply this to strangers as well, and it's easier with them—they have no expectations of who I am, and therefore ask fewer questions. If I see a fight in a bar, for instance, I either try to talk the sparring parties down—to be a bridge—or to simply stand close by and set my mental energy on a feeling of peace and understanding by emptying my mind of all concrete thought, inhaling deeply and exhaling minimally. It's a fasting of breath until a more harmonious external state is reached. People may look at me like, "What's this weirdo doing here?" but they say nothing, and I believe it makes them think. Makes them see this alternative way of being is possible and real.

But when I went home last weekend, and Rachel dropped me off at the end of the night, I left a card for her on the passenger's seat. It read, "You are beautiful, inside and out. You are a true friend. I will always love you, and I believe that you can do anything you set your heart to in this life."

When I got back to school the next night, she wrote to me on instant messenger: "Are you okay?"

I asked her what she meant.

"You just seem different," she wrote. "Like something's wrong. Like something happened to you. Did something happen?"

I sat there, tense, and stared at the screen. My commitment to honesty and clarity, to true communication, obliged me to think of the most accurate possible answer to this question. What, if anything, could be wrong?

"If I had to pinpoint something," I wrote, "I guess it was this weird incident with this guy."

I told her, then, about Andy. It was a humiliating admission, in a way, because really I should be over it—and in some ways I am. I even apply my precepts to him. Every couple months or so, I instant message him—things like "You seem smart," or "You have a nice smile," or "I hope you find happiness in life." When he doesn't respond, I must admit, it makes me angry—but I'm able to fight through that anger by understanding that the stakes are much higher than this momentary feeling of embarrassment. Putting the positive message out there is what matters. I need him to know that I understand. I don't hold anything against him. I remember that photo of his mom, the way he patted that spot on the couch at Matty's all those months ago, with a friendly smile on his face, and I believe that he is a good person who ultimately means well.

"Oh, that?" she wrote. "I hate to say it, my friend, but that's just what guys do in college."

And there it was. My unawareness, my oversensitivity—it smacked me in the face like debris in a windstorm.

I was twelve years old again—alone and foolish, abnormal and exposed.

When I'm through with my banana, I rise to my feet and step to the nearby trash can, where I drop the emptied peel and watch it flail down into the darkness of the barrel. The ground beneath me as I walk toward the dorm is cushiony, soft, and not wholly supportive, morphing and mushing and swaying me back and forth. It's a feeling I once relished as a little girl trying to walk inside a Bouncy House, in a breathless rapture as, try as I might to stay upright and move forward, I slipped down off my feet. But this is no Bouncy House, this is so-called life I'm supposed to be living, and it is somehow not happening. I'm outside of it all. A thick cloud hangs between me and the physical world. The ground beneath my feet, the banana peel I just watched fall into the garbage can, the faces of the people I pass, the Gothic buildings I once coveted so much surrounding me like towering, ghastly beasts casting me sinister smiles—it's all slipping farther and farther away, and I wonder if now is the time. If now, even as I walk, is the time when I am in fact starting to die.

My phone vibrates in my backpack. I pull it out and see that it's Steve. Of course now he would call. This tells me something, about the universe—

"Hello?" I say, my voice accusing.

"Woah. Hello? Rinie?"

"Yes."

"What's wrong?"

"Nothing."

"You sound funny."

"What?"

"You sound crazy. You're crazy."

"I'm not crazy!"

"Who said you were?"

"You did! You just said, 'You sound crazy. You're crazy.'"

"No, I didn't. I said you sound *funny.*"

"You're lying! You said I sound crazy!"

"Rinie, Rinie, get a grip. I did not say you sound crazy."

My hands shake, my eyelids flutter. More quietly, I say, "You did. You just said . . ."

"I didn't say crazy, Rinie. I didn't." His voice is soft, almost apologetic in its gentleness.

"But I heard you say it. You said it! You're lying. You're trying to *make* me crazy!"

"Rinie, I . . ."

I hang up and walk faster now. I need to lie down, to slow the cogs in my mind that are churning out new thoughts and ideas and ways of seeing myself, the world, and others at a rate of productivity far too rapid for me to adequately manage—see, sort, and allocate—the output.

I stop at Lymon Hall to use the ladies' room. I paper the toilet seat in the first stall and sit, elbows on my knees, hands gripping my temples. I expect to feel blood, or something else, something worse, some sign of death, gushing out, but nothing happens. I look up and see a poster on the stall door. In large bold letters at the top of the page, it reads, "Was It Rape?"

No, I think, my head ticking back and forth like a metronome turned up too high. *No it wasn't.*

"Did you know?" it reads, and then in smaller font below, a bullet point: "Many victims of rape believe that rape only happens to bad people."

My heart pounds, and I feel the veins in my arms swelling up; I am immobile, stuck, in every way possible—body and mind.

"Did you say no?" it reads across the middle of the page.

"Yes," I say in a low voice, "I did."

"Did he listen?"

But I didn't say it loud enough. I didn't push him hard enough. I was there, in his bed. I was kissing him . . .

"Wearing a sexy outfit is not a rapeable offense," it lists at the bottom.

I know that, I think. *I wasn't even wearing a sexy outfit . . .*

"Having too many drinks is not a rapeable offense," it continues. "Kissing is not a rapeable offense."

It's not?

It's not! You should know *that. If it were anyone else in that situation, you would* know *that.*

"Get Help," it reads in large letters across the bottom, along with a phone number and other information I can't process.

"There's no one who can help me," I say aloud.

When I step down the front stairs of Lymon, all I can feel is an urgent need to get back to my dorm room; I need to drink water, and to lie down. I'm tempted to lie there on the grass, but I push myself onward through the thick fog. The air, the whole atmosphere surrounding me, appears black, while the trees and buildings and people are all shining out in bright, fluorescent shades, like magnified atoms in space, or figments of my imagination, or fragments of memory, because maybe I'm already dead.

Through the fog, a face bursts through. It is Andy's.

"Hey," he calls, and smiles, from fifty feet away. This itself—his appearance in this moment—is to me another sign that a powerful hand is at play. He seems to be shouting, waving, running at me, bearing down like a bison in an open, empty field. I feel no capacity to respond, to change my pace or make use of my voice; my legs continue their pace, but I am otherwise frozen—my eyes, mouth, cheeks: nothing will move. The smile, seemingly hysterical, on his face is melting as he continues to watch me pass. The corners of his mouth narrow, his eyebrows scrunch, his pupils pull downward and left. In confusion? Hurt? Fear? Do I, now, too, look like a monster? I stare him in the eyes and see a boy dressed up as a man, and I know in that moment that that's what we all are—just children, pretending. The part of me that wants to say or do something, to smile and wave and somehow ameliorate whatever has caused this—pained?—expression on his face, is powerless beneath a debilitating stillness that's set down on me, even as my body moves forward. My gaze is set on his face and I sense that this is the last instant in my life in which I will see that face, his face, at least outside my mind, and at last, I realize it doesn't matter; I don't care.

For an English class, I read an essay called "The Crack-up," by F. Scott Fitzgerald—the same guy who wrote *The Great Gatsby*. In it, he said, "*The test of a first-rate intelligence is the ability to hold two opposing ideas in mind at the same time and still retain the ability to function.*" But what if one holds more than two opposing ideas? What if one holds three or four or ten, all at once, each wrestling for prominence throughout the course of one day, within the relatively small space of one mind? What is the opposite of "to function"?

Fitzgerald says "to crack."

I reach the dorm room with no sense of how I got there and push desperately on the unlocked door, with no patience for it. I collapse onto the futon in our living room. Kathryn sweeps in from the bedroom a few minutes later, sees me, and says, "You don't look so good." She asks if I need some Tylenol, water—am I going to vomit?

"No," I say. "Just . . . feel dizzy, weak. I'm nauseous and achy. My back hurts."

"Eek," she says, cracking open a can of soda. "What if you have meningitis?"

I shift the pillow that covers my face to peek up at her. "What's that?"

135

She rolls her eyes. "You don't know what meningitis is?"

"Well, I've *heard* of it." *What makes her so smart?* "I just don't really know what it is . . . the symptoms?"

She shrugs. "Pretty much what you said. Nausea, weakness, achiness." She takes a long swig of her drink. "It's very common among college students. Affects the spinal cord."

The spinal cord. Nerves. *My arms do feel prickly.* "No, it can't be meningitis. I just need rest."

She shrugs again and tosses her half-full can into the trash, then slips her lip gloss out from her pocket and smothers it onto her lips. "Well." She rubs them together and smacks them loudly into a pucker. "I'm off. The girls and I are going out for some last-day-of-class cocktails. Hope you feel better!"

"Thanks," I grumble.

She slides past me, grabs her purse from the coffee table, and walks out the door. I roll over and off the futon and head for the bedroom, where I sit on my bed, turn on my computer, and type "meningitis" into Google.

The symptom list: Nausea, *check*. Back pain, *check*. Headache, pretty much *check*. Fever—I feel my forehead—possibly *check*. Rapid breathing—*yes;* that's been a constant for months. Change in mental status—*what?*

The phrase is blue and underlined, a hyperlink. I click on it and see it is defined—"State: Disorientation. Thinking: Unclear. Thoughts: Cloudy."

My breathing quickens more rapidly now as I reach for my phone and press, "Home."

"Hello?" It's my mother who answers, sounding breathless as well, as if she had run to the phone from across the house.

"Mom."

"Rinie, what's the matter?"

"Mom, I think I have meningitis."

"What? Why would you think that?"

"Well, because I feel nauseous, and my back hurts, and my roommate says those are symptoms of meningitis, and I'm a college student, and . . ."

"That's ridiculous. Why would she say that?"

"I looked it up online, and it's true. She's right."

"Well, did you *eat* anything today?"

I think of what I did eat today; the banana?

"Yes, I did."

"Are you *sure?*"

"Yes, yes, Mom, please!"

"Rinie, you do not have meningitis. You would *know* if you had meningitis."

A strange and sudden feeling of calm settles over me. The room falls into a peaceful silence, as if a blasting stereo has just been powered off, or a loud and speeding train has come to a halt. "Are you sure?" I whisper. It's painful to be so vulnerable with my mother. The last thing I want is for her to see me weak, in need. I don't like to think of her worrying about me. She worries enough. And yet it feels so good to hear her voice, steady and firm, benevolently harsh.

"I am *sure,*" she continues. "Though if you aren't feeling well, go to the health center and get checked out. But Rinie, again, if you had meningitis, I think you would know."

Would I? "You really think so?"

"I do." The words are as reassuring as they must be to a bride. "But go to the health center and get checked out, just for peace of mind. And for goodness sakes, get some rest, honey."

I *feel* like honey now, warm and sweet, as I hang up the phone and wonder why I don't reach for my mother more often.

But before I can decide what to do about the health center, my phone rings again. It is Steve, who wants to know if I'm okay; he'd been worried about me earlier.

"Steve, we really can't talk anymore. Like, at all," I say. "It isn't fair to you."

"How many times do I have to say this? Can't I be the one who decides what's fair to me?"

"But I'm telling you that we will never be together that way again. It's just not going to happen."

He's silent for a moment. "That's what worries me, Rinie. I'm worried about you. I'm worried that if we don't end up together, you'll . . ."

"I'll what?" *I'll end up alone forever? I'll die? What does he know that I don't?*

"I just worry," he says. "That's all."

The comfort I'd felt from speaking with my mother is suddenly gone, and the pressing, pulsing fear has returned. I know, now, that I will pick up the phone the next time that he calls.

I fall into a deep, dark, cavernous sleep in which I dream of being trapped inside a car, rolling backward down a hill toward a ravine. I wake to see Kathryn's face as it hovers above me.

"Rinie, Rinie, wake up," she hisses, smiling, giggling, shaking my shoulder like she's sifting sugar.

"Kathryn?" My eyes slit open to see her.

"Yes, it's Kathryn, silly. Get up! Come hang out with me!"

I glance at the clock. "Is it really 1 a.m.?"

Her head swivels in a circular motion. "It's *really* 1 a.m.," she drones. "You're so weird, Rinie. Why wouldn't it be 1 a.m.?"

I rub my eyes. "Are you okay, Kathryn?"

"Of course I'm okay!" She pokes her finger into my chest bone. "Are *you* okay?"

"I'm . . . fine, a little better."

She waves her hand in the air. "Whatever. I hope so." She

places a hand on my desk to steady the swaying. "You have been so wild these past few months. Drinking all the time, smoking pot . . . and here I thought you were this innocent Little Miss Goody Two-Shoes." She stops to indulge in a laugh. Her body breezes about like a birch tree in the wind. She smiles a devious smile, and then swoops down toward my face to lean in close, uncomfortably close. Then presses her lips onto mine. I turn my head to the right and try to pretend I didn't notice, but she cackles and shouts, "I was trying to *kiss* you, Rinie. On the *mouth!*"

I scrunch back toward the wall and offer a slight laugh. "Oh, come on, Kathryn. You're drunk and being silly." Tomorrow, Kathryn—dear, pretty Kathryn with her trust fund and manners, her powerful lawyer parents and heiress friends—will wake up humiliated, and I want to normalize the situation as much as possible.

But Kathryn continues: "I'm serious. I tried to *kiss* you, like, for real." She sways backward. "Don't pretend like you didn't notice. You're not so naïve!" She pulls out my desk chair and sits with a hard thump. "But I know. You're scared. That night you got in bed with me, I saw how scared you were. I wanted to help you." She shakes her head. "I don't understand girls like you. Why you're so afraid to own that word, *rape*. I guess because once you own it, you've gotta do something about it. And it doesn't seem like that's your thing, is it? Doing something about it. But you know what else? That bastard Andy is *disgusting*. What he did to you was *disgusting*. I am *not* sorry I told him off. You have been acting like a total *doormat*." Her head swings side to side and she repeats, "No, I am *not* sorry."

The ceiling, once again, closes down on me. I say, with whatever sound I can extract from my throat, "Kathryn, you need to go to bed. You're drunk."

"I am *not* drunk." She points a finger in the air. "But even if

I was! You know I'm right. You *know* . . ." Again, she reaches down and pokes me in the chest bone, leans in close to my face, her lips near mine. "I'm right."

Those months ago, when I'd gotten into her bed—what made me think that was okay? Because she was a girl? Again, I'd gotten into someone's bed, feeling safe. Again, I'd been un-fair, sending the wrong signals. Again, I am faced with the awareness that I have absolutely no idea what to do with myself in this life. I have no idea how to communicate with others. I have no idea what is true and right.

And I also, probably, have meningitis.

Once Kathryn retires to bed, and I can safely hear her snor-ing, I rise and dress and march across campus to the 24-hour student health center, like a renegade traveler, the stars my only witnesses. When the lady at reception asks me what the prob-lem is, I tell her, "Meningitis. I think I have meningitis."

She looks up from beneath her glasses and simply says, "Fill this out," as she hands me a clipboard of forms.

Ten minutes later, I sit on a wax-papered table in a cold examination room as a nurse, a small blonde woman who asks to be called Jenny, takes my temperature, checks my reflexes, shines a light into my eyes and ears, and draws my blood. I en-joy the sensation of this, her attending to each part of me, these parts I rarely think of. My ears? Could all of this trouble be in those ears? In my eyes? Could all of it be solved with a quick cold knock on the knees?

"Have you gotten much sleep lately?" Nurse Jenny asks as she works.

"Yes and no," I say in a shaky voice, and she marks a note on her clipboard.

"And what made you think you have meningitis?" She

squeezes on the blood pressure pump.

"I don't know. My symptoms, I guess." The pressure around my arm releases, and she jots another note, then stops her tinkering to look me in the face. "It's not likely that you have meningitis."

I'm surprised to feel something inside of me sink in disappointment. I am tired of wondering when the bomb will go off. The prospect of lying in a bed, under care, without having to move around and do things and speak to other people, was appealing, and really, I've been working so hard. It may not seem like work to other people, but it *is* work. It *is*.

"Would you like to stay here for the night?" Jenny asks, and I am thankful that she can read my mind; I wonder what I did to deserve such a gift. Every muscle in my body loosens. "Until your blood work comes in?"

"Can I?"

"You can. We can have someone bring over your books."

I stay for three days. When the good people working in the health center ask if I need or want my books, I say no; I can study for my finals later, I'm all caught up. They offer me a magazine, a sweet and thoughtless magazine. I haven't read one in years. I say, "Sure," and I flip through the pages, glancing at the pictures without registering a word. They offer me Gatorade, which feels like the most kind and generous gesture I have ever received, and I thank them for it, over and over, until they start giving me funny looks.

The last days of school pass by swiftly. After three glorious days on the soft, remote health center bed, I take my exams and, on my last day at school, I sit in a coffee shop and write goodbye notes to Kathryn, Jasmine, Daniella, and even Agnes. For each one, I personalize a note—

"Kathryn, I admire how focused you are, and how you take an active role in trying to help others; I know you will be a great success in life."

"Jasmine, you are a fun and good-hearted person. I know that you will always be surrounded by friends and love."

"Daniella, you have the lightest, most open spirit of anyone I have met at this school."

"Agnes, you are a bold and independent spirit, and I admire you."

I know they will, at best, roll their eyes and laugh at me for these notes; at worst, they will share them with others and have a big, more public laugh at my expense. But it doesn't matter. Some things need to be said, and I can't worry too much about my own ego anymore, unless it's in service of something better. So to everyone, I conclude with the same note of gratitude: *"Thank you for teaching me so much about myself. I promise to try to put it to good use. And thank you for being you."*

I even type that in an instant message to Andy. But I delete the last sentence and just send the first two.

CHAPTER TEN
AGE NINETEEN - THE SUMMER BEFORE

"Pin it open," Grandma said, "to what you wrote."

On a late August afternoon, a few weeks before I moved on campus, I stood in my Grandma Ginny's hospital room before the bulletin board opposite her bed, searching for an empty space to hang the card I'd brought. "But you can't even read the words from back there," I said. "The picture on the front is cute. These kittens cuddling."

I bought the card at a CVS pharmacy across the street from the hospital, where I had visited my grandmother almost every day that summer. But this night, I felt I should bring something with me. In part, it was because I felt guilty about the fact that my trip in and out would be quick. I had plans to go out that night—a sort of conditioning for the lifestyle that lay ahead of me at college. I hastily selected the first blank card that caught my eye—one with the image of two tiger-striped tabby cats nestling together—and I hustled out to the car, where I dug a pencil out from the glove compartment and scribbled, under the rearview mirror light, the first words that appeared in my mind: *Grandma, you have a faith like no one else I know. I know you're going to be better really soon.*

It was a way not to lie. *Better* could mean anything.

"Rinie," Grandma replied. "Could you please just pin it open?"

I felt shy about having my words on display like that, for

anyone to see. But this persistence from Grandma was so unusual that I had to agree, "If you say so."

"Thank you," she said, nodding in rhythm, in the way that she did—her eyes set on her lap, seeming to stare at nothing of this world; at some strange idea or concern that the nodding helped her to cope with.

"So what else can I do?" Hands on hips, I surveyed the room, with its bright white, concrete walls, plotting the rearrangement of plants, balloons, and stuffed animals. "What do you think about moving this fern over there, by the window?"

"Rinie." Her head still nodded steadily in rhythm but her gray eyes now set squarely on me.

"What's up?" I said, scanning the room.

"Rinie, when I die . . ." She emphasized the word *die* with a deep nod, as if to push the word out.

"Grandma," I said, "don't talk like that."

"When I *die*," she repeated, with palpable struggle; she hated to ask for anything. "I want you to remember me. I want you to remember . . . that you're not just Greek."

I rolled my eyes. "How can I forget something like that? That's like forgetting my eyes are brown."

"I want you to remember, though, and think about it. And think about me, too. Remember how I am." She put a finger to the corner of each eye. "I don't want you to be like me."

I didn't understand the comment. What was so wrong with *her?*

She'd had a challenging life; I'd always known that. She'd been poor, and ill—with cancer, but also "nerves," my mom used to say. Nerves. Yes, Grandma had always seemed *nervous*.

And of course there were her marriages. Three of them. Back on the horse three times, each with visions of what? Happily ever after? Safety? Understanding?

But late in life, Grandma Ginny seemed happy on her own,

144

in her little senior-community apartment that smelled consistently of Pine Sol and bleach. She enjoyed her routines and rituals, the cleanliness and simplicity of her habits.

And Grandma was kind. Truly, to her core, selfless. Wasn't that a good thing? Wasn't it a virtue?

"Please, Grandma, that's crazy. What are you saying? Don't be silly."

"I'm serious, Rinie. I want you to hear me."

"I hear you, Grandma, but I don't like what I'm hearing." I walked to her bedside table and fumbled with the remote control. "Let's put some TV on. Why don't you relax?"

The rhythmic nodding began again as she stared not at the television but at the wall. "I love you, Rinie. Come give me a kiss. You can go off with your friends now. You don't need to sit in here with an old lady like me." She waved a hand and smiled serenely. "Go."

Hundreds of times I'd heard her say this, and it always seemed so silly. I *liked* spending time with her.

But this time, she was right—I didn't want to be in that hospital room, with her dying plants and requests, with the stench of disinfectant reminding me of frog dissection day in Biology class; with the sun, whose warmth she'd never directly feel again, shining its light through the wall-to-wall windows that couldn't be opened.

"Oh stop," I said, badly feigning sincerity.

"Go, Miss Rinie. Really. I want you to go and have fun."

"Are you sure?"

"Yes, go. Have a good night. And *please* be careful."

I smiled and rolled my eyes. "Grandma, you *always* say be careful; I always *am* careful."

Grandma brushed her blanket. "I always *want* you to be careful."

I contorted my body around the tubes and wires and leaned

in to find the one square inch of skin exposed to kiss her cheek. "Okay, Grandma," I sang. "I'll be careful. I love you, too. I'll see you tomorrow." I walked toward the doorway and turned to wave and smile. "Bye, Grandma."

"Goodbye, Rinie."

The next day, she was in a coma. The day after that she was gone.

"She's gone," my mother said into the phone that morning, between sobs. "Grandma's gone, Rinie. I'm sorry."

She said it, "I'm sorry," as if it were somehow her fault. I could hear her take a deep drag off a cigarette and it annoyed me. Then, in a voice more stable, she said, "Are you okay?"

I was in the hallway between my bedroom and the bathroom. As she asked me this, I leaned against the wall and blinked, in that heavy way where you can feel and not ignore the feel of your eyelids clamping down. "I'm okay, Mom." I took a deep breath and asked what I didn't want to know: "Are you okay?"

She inhaled—another drag. "I'm fine."

"I'll come to the hospital . . ."

"No, no, don't. We'll be leaving soon. We'll see you later. Rinie, are you okay?"

"I'm okay."

"Okay. Bye."

I flipped my phone shut, held it out in front of me, and stared at it for a long moment, then pulled my arm back and flung it down to the carpeted floor, with enough force for it to bounce up and over the banister. I watched it fall to the foyer below and, as it smacked the tile, something inside me released, like gas from a faulty valve.

I stared at the phone lying there below, then closed my eyes and breathed in deep, clenching my fists and growling a deep growl. My legs moved in rapid strides down the stairs and toward the phone. I picked it up and saw, through the cracked screen, some faded gray numbers: "9:11." My fingers began dialing numbers, pressing hard into each button, as if someone had taken over my body, listening with satisfaction for each beep of the keys as I dialed Steve's number.

We were already broken up then, but I called him anyway. I heard his voice say, "Rinie?" And another voice, mine, came out in a wail.

"She's gone! My grandma died. I can't believe she *died!* I didn't really think she would *die.* How can she be gone? I just saw her yesterday, she's *gone!*"

He said in a low voice, "Calm down, Rinie. It's okay."

"But it doesn't make *sense!* She was *here,* and now she's *gone.* And I'm here, you're here, and her body's there, just like yesterday, but it's different . . . how am I—how is anyone—supposed to understand the *difference?*"

"It's okay, Rinie. It's going to be okay."

"It's not okay, though!" I shouted, so loudly that it staggered me, and I fell back to sit on the stairs. "There's no such *thing* as okay! It's just an illusion, this idea that we're ever, any of us, *okay*—because we're all just killing time until the next catastrophe. There's just no point! It'll never be okay, none of it, just like it's never been okay that Mark died, either!"

There was silence, then. I'd never mentioned my dead brother to him—he'd only learned about him through Eugenia—and I made it clear the topic was off limits. "Rinie, I'm sorry . . ." he started to say.

"No," I shook my head. "I'm sorry. I shouldn't have called you. It was wrong."

"I'm glad you called me . . ."

"No, no, I told you we were over, and that we shouldn't

talk anymore, that we weren't going to work."

"Rinie, stop. I always told you to call if you needed me. I'm glad you called . . ."

"You don't understand. I shouldn't have called. I'm an idiot. A weak fucking idiot. I'm sorry." I rattled my head. "Thank you, but I'm sorry. I have to go." I hung up the phone and sat on the stairs staring at nothing until I heard a key in the lock of the front door. Then I ran upstairs and hid under the covers.

I insisted on speaking at the funeral. My mother tried to tell me it wasn't necessary, that an older cousin from the other side of the family could easily do it, but it had to be me, I said. That morning, I woke up at 6:00 a.m. and took a jog around the neighborhood. When I returned home, I toasted myself a slice of whole grain bread, smeared it with a dab of strawberry jam, and gulped down a cold glass of ice water and a four-ounce glass of orange juice.

The whole house was silent while the rest of my family slept. I creaked open the patio door and nibbled on my bread, tuning into the sound of the chirping birds—unnaturally loud chirping, it seemed.

A few hours later, the family lined up in the front pew at the church, each of us dressed in all black. Wearing black stockings, a black skirt, black shoes, and a black sweater, I felt appropriately dark against the warm, brown wood.

As Grandma Ginny's casket rolled down the aisle, I had to stifle a laugh. It felt silly, absurd, all that pomp and circumstance for Grandma. She would have been mortified by the attention—a packed church watching her body, lain out and, albeit covered by a box, displayed for all to see; and meanwhile, this solemn, ceremonious violin music playing in the background.

Too much. It was all too much. None of this helped me feel . . . the gravity of what it was all supposed to mean.

So I stared at the altar, at the gold and blue stitching on the cloth draped over the table. I traced the loops along the bottom, to see if they would link up with the ones along the side and connect all the way around; I studied the recurrence in the designs at the center—the golden crosses, each circumscribed by a large clover with diamonds affixed to its four outermost points. I was in the midst of counting them, ensuring— pleading for—balance in the design, when I heard the priest announce my name. He gave me a private look, head cocked to one side, eyebrows raised, as if to ask, "Do you still want to do this?"

I felt angered by this soft-gloved touch. I said I would speak, and I would.

I walked up to the podium, where I unfolded the sheet of loose-leaf paper with frayed edges and penciled scribblings. Into the microphone, I spoke in a voice I didn't recognize, much louder, yet thinner than usual. "My grandmother was the most selfless person I have ever known . . ."

As I continued reading, it felt as though I were screaming, or scolding, the way I enunciated each word, but I couldn't stop doing it. My eyes blazed through the paper as I didn't look up once, and I could hear my own voice speaking words as if they were someone else's; as if I were someone else.

I swallowed hard before reading the closing lines. Then, with a feeling of superhuman strength—or something more, and other than strength—I said, "My grandma's biggest fear was that I'd end up just like her. But mine is that I won't."

It felt ominous, but true. I looked up, then, at the audience, as if they'd just appeared. I smiled through closed lips and took my seat.

Afterward, I was inundated with praise from family and friends. "How wonderful!" "How sweet!" "How poised you were up there!" I nodded and smiled and thanked them and said, "It was easy. I just told the truth." But I had this funny feeling, now, since I'd spoken; as if some force had grabbed hold of me from the time I began writing that speech until that very moment in the narthex when I'd said, "It was easy," when the force had let me go. I was on my own.

A week later, I packed up Grandma's vacuum, dishes, and silverware and brought them with me to school as an offering to my new communal living space. Kathryn was "so sorry to hear" that my grandma had passed, but I waved my hand and said, "Oh, that's all right"—not that it was really all right, but because I didn't feel that Grandma died the way other grandmas did, as in the natural order of things. I wanted to dismiss the standard cordialities that might make it so. Grandma and I were closer than that—so close that she could still give me things that a living person would; practical things like cleaning supplies and utensils, so I "would be okay up there at the college."

I could almost hear her saying that. And so my roommate saying she was sorry made me think, perhaps for a moment too long, to call Grandma and have a good laugh with her about how silly that seemed.

CHAPTER ELEVEN
ONE YEAR LATER - THE FOLLOWING MAY

When Grandma got the chance, she brought me Lucas.

Perched on her cloud in Heaven, she surveyed the land—or, at least, the Boston metro area—and found him in a little apartment on the outskirts of the city, in a neighborhood called Allston.

I met him where I work, at the Higher Grounds coffee shop in Kenmore Square. It's a fun spot, on the second floor of a historic townhouse-style building up the road from the subway station. I was on a break, at a corner table, reading a book while intermittently staring out the bay window at the street below, when I spotted him climbing the steps and entering the shop.

He was tall, at least six feet, and wore a navy blue Red Sox cap with faded green cargo pants, dress shoes, and a short-sleeved button-down shirt. A young man at work. But there was something about his walk, the way his shoulders sloped down, with his arms hung loose and lanky at his sides; the way he stared straight ahead as he walked, two piercing blue eyes flashing out like beams of light beneath the rim of that hat . . .

I felt a discomforting twinge of interest in this man. When he entered the shop, the chimes above the door rang out, and it made me smile. He looked right at me—practically through me—with eyes that paused on my face for half a second too long, and then refocused themselves on the line to buy a coffee.

On his way out of the store a few minutes later, I sensed his eyes on me again but wouldn't turn my face. And that was the whole of our first encounter.

But the next day, the same thing happened, at the same time of day—he walked in while I was on break. I watched as he stood in line, his arms folded laxly across his chest, suggesting a faint vulnerability at odds with that cavernous aura, and the confident voice that spoke to me moments later when he approached my table and said, "Hi. I'm Lucas. Do you mind if I sit down?"

In many ways, the conditions of my life had improved by the time I met Lucas. Last May, after completing my junior year, I left quietly for home in Rhode Island to a summer of waitressing and breathing and slowly mending the frays of my existence. I met Lucas when I was about to graduate, with grades that nudged up into the mid-B range—not quite the straight As of my first two years, but not the low Cs and dropped classes of the third year, either. The Political Science major I dropped once and for all, and I was finishing up my English major with a course on the Transcendentalists. I worked three days a week at Higher Grounds, which gave me some extra money and a feeling of responsibility, normalcy.

Most grounding of all, though, has been the fact that I've been living in an 11th floor apartment on Commonwealth Avenue with Eugenia, who returned to Boston this fall for a job. Our place is a couple miles—a healthy distance—from campus, and through my bedroom window I can see the reservoir. Most weeknights we spend watching television, eating carrot sticks and pretzels dipped in low-fat hummus, and making each other laugh. Some nights during the school year, especially when Eugenia would go out, I holed up in my room to paint. I took a painting class in my last semester, just for fun; mostly, I'd just swirl some colors around, tossing in some random shapes and patterns. After the final for the class, Eugenia and I hung my paintings around the living room and hosted a mock exhibit for her boyfriend, Salim, a used car dealer from Lebanon, who was willing to play along. We wore pajamas and slippers, and we sipped cheap wine and nibbled on crackers and fruit splayed out on the coffee table as I described my inspiration and process for each piece in an affected, haughty tone.

So by the time I met Lucas, I was in a safer, if not better, place compared to the year before.

In a way, I missed the wildness, that raw and reckless abandon. It had brought me to life in a way I hadn't expected, awakening dormant parts of my brain and heart. But even if, in my senior year, I felt subdued and slightly apathetic, I was more securely balanced. I could see and hear and think more clearly, more *normally*, as measured against the mainstream population. My grip on my emotions and perceptions was firmer . . .

Yet tenuous, always on the verge of regression.

For instance, on an early Friday morning in March, on a day I didn't have class or anything else to do but clean my apartment, I was out at the local Star Market, stocking up on glass cleaner and bleach—I like to keep things spic-and-span—when I entirely lost my car. I'd parked it in a spot directly out front, with (I thought) enough money loaded into the meter, but I left the store to find the car gone. *Where did I park?* I wondered—a normal thought, which quickly devolved: *Didn't I park here? Did I park here? Did I park anywhere, or did I walk here?*

Did they tow my car?

Why would they tow my car? I paid the meter. Did I pay the meter? Is this a legal spot?

Am I losing my mind? Again?

153

Why is this happening to me? What have I done so wrong in this world? What does this mean? What is the universe trying to tell me? Why does it hate me so goddamn much?

It was a police officer who broke my train of thought. "Ma'am?" he said. "Are you looking for your car?"

"Yes," I breathed.

"Your car has been towed," he confirmed. With hands on hips, he shifted his weight backward. "Too many outstanding tickets."

Outstanding tickets? I hadn't gotten any tickets lately.

The world began swirling around me, and I became a smudge of color streaked across it.

In order to retrieve my car from the lot to which it had been towed, I had to go to the Westmore City Hall to pay the unpaid fines. "They're cracking down," the woman in the bursar's office said. "Didn't you read about it in the paper?"

The paper? "I didn't know anything about it," I said, in a daze. "I haven't gotten a ticket in forever."

The lady snorted. "How long's forever? You got a long lista tickets here, honey. Adding up to two thousand dollars and change." Martha, according to her name plate, printed off the receipt, the sharp tick-ticking sound grating my every nerve. She put on her tiny glasses and spread the long, thin slip of paper across the counter. "See here? They start in November 2002 and go up to . . . May 2003. Looks like you got a ticket almost every day from February onward." She peeked up at me above the rim of her glasses. "Boy!"

With every word from Martha, I felt the weight of gravity sucking my body downward. How could I have blocked this memory out? It seemed like eons ago—like a completely different life, a different person, so much so that the city of Westmore should have somehow known this and seen in an instant that this criminal was someone else, in another lifetime, in a parallel world that no longer existed, and everything that took place in that parallel world should no longer remain in any sort of collective consciousness, memory, or system of record-keeping.

But the city wanted its money, from one Irinie Pothos, and my car would not be returned until that one Irinie Pothos paid up.

I had no choice, it seemed, but to call my father.

"*Two thousand dollars?*" he shouted into the phone. "I don't understand. How does a person get two thousand dollars in tickets?"

"I know, I know. It's hard to explain." I closed my eyes to summon the strength—or weakness—of an alternate self. "I really wish I didn't have to ask you this, but they are holding my car until I pay. I have a thousand dollars saved, but I need another thousand."

He sighed. "A thousand dollars you worked so hard for, and now you gonna throw it away like this." When I said nothing, he continued. "When do you need it?"

Through gritted teeth, I said, "Today."

A painful silence, so I went on: "I'll pay you back every single cent. I'll come home every weekend to work at the diner. I'll pay you back in no time."

"I don't know how you did this." His voice was eerily calm. "It's not the money, it's the principle."

I knew that. I knew that he would gladly give me any money he could for a good reason. The way I'd avoided, all through college, even asking him for five dollars, for *one* dollar, all that pride—all of it had been rendered absurd, with one swift phone call saying, "I need a thousand dollars right now."

After that, I went home almost every weekend, as promised, to work at the diner. It was for the best, anyway. That ticket fiasco set me in the wrong direction on my internal redemption meter—an unofficial tally I maintained in my mind of all the good and bad things I did, to ensure that the needle tipped farther toward the good. Going home kept me confined, regimented; responsibility kept me safe from mistakes.

Lucas and I learned the basic facts about each other that day on my break. He had graduated from the University of New Hampshire the year before and was working for a pet products distributor—a fact I adored—right there in Kenmore Square.

"What are you gonna do after graduation?" he asked me.

It was a question I heard a lot those days, and I generally responded with things like, "I don't know, maybe grad school, or maybe I'll work for a nonprofit, or write for a magazine." But that day, an idea flashed into my mind like a blaze of sunlight. "I might go live in Greece for a while," I said.

He said that was cool, and that he had tentative plans to move, too, to Colorado with his friends when his company opened an office there in the fall.

That made it easier to accept a first date with him. How serious could things get, with both of us, apparently, moving?

Our first date was on a Saturday morning in Cambridge. It had been three days since I last saw him, but it felt more like three years. The image of his face, his stance, that chasmal expression—I couldn't get it out of my mind. When I saw him, it felt like seeing a good friend I hadn't seen in a while, and I had to remind myself that I barely knew him.

I met him by a lamppost near the Central Square T station. He wore a bright yellow T-shirt with a strange black symbol on it that looked either like a peace sign or a palm tree. He was listening to music on his headphones as he scanned the crowd, a *Boston Phoenix* newspaper tucked under his arm. When I came running up from the underground station, he was the first thing I saw, and he smiled immediately—with relief, it seemed, as his whole body relaxed. "You made it," he said.

It was 10:45 in the morning, I know, because I was fifteen minutes late, apologetic as ever, though I admitted to him that I was actually almost always like this—late and apologizing. My mom was the same way, and so was her father, and his mother, and so it wasn't really a gender thing, but definitely somewhat genetic. I was rambling, which I didn't expect to do, but there was something about him that made me want to talk and talk.

"You don't need to apologize," he said. "I'm just glad you're here."

He pulled me into a hug. My face pressed into his chest and the soft cotton of his T-shirt. He smelled like an oak tree if you pushed your nose up to the bark in early spring and the scent mixed in with the fresh-cut grass—it was an earthy smell, verdant, as if he himself were a form of plant life, green and new.

I wanted to linger there in that moment, with the volume of our breathing turned up high, but I extracted myself with some effort.

"So . . ." I said.

"So." He smiled shyly, and it felt like I could see right through the yellow shirt he wore, right through his skin and bones into some sort of inner core, as if his body were inverted. "I thought maybe we'd take a walk?" he said.

We walked for miles, through Cambridge, then across the bridge to Boston, through Quincy Market and the North End, by the waterfront, through Back Bay, and past Fenway Park, where I confessed that I'd never been to a baseball game.

"There's a lot of this stuff," I told him. "I've never seen *Star Wars*. Never been in a canoe . . ."

"You've never seen *Star Wars?* You've never been in a canoe?" he said, in barely-feigned horror. "Well, I'll personally make sure you accomplish both of those things by the end of the summer."

If I'd been able to detach from the moment, that statement—the thought of making plans through the summer—would have spawned a small fit of anxiety. But I wasn't; able to detach, that is. I didn't really want to.

From there, the summer has spread into a long stream of semiconscious moments, interrupted only by the occasional obvious question: "What happens when the summer is over?"

Since my casual comment about moving to Greece those months ago, the idea has become a real possibility. My tentative plan is to stay with Yiayia. She would enjoy the company. I'll work somewhere on the island and spend all of my free time by the ocean or hiking up mountains and writing in my journal—finding myself; figuring out what I'm meant to do with my life.

My parents don't love the idea—they think I should get a traditional job, or go to grad school, or do something "normal." But what can they say? My father left his home country at age eighteen.

At the same time, though, Lucas and I have begun to talk, somewhat kiddingly, about moving out West together. The thought of moving there with him, somewhere new for both of us, is unwaveringly appealing. When a day spent with Lucas ends, I look forward to the next with an urgency I can't suppress. Even when I'm alone, I have a hard time *feeling* alone.

But I don't want to fall into the trap of just changing my plans and following a man. That isn't who I am, or want to be.

He delivered, for the most part, on his promise about the canoe. He took me to the Berkshire Hills last week, for a trip down the Housatonic, though we kayaked instead. "I think you'll like having your own boat to paddle," he said on the way up there, and I'd taken to trusting him on matters like this.

We rented our boats and paddled down a five-mile stretch of the river that was, for the most part, very tame. On either side were hills flush with trees, blanketed by sunlight; above us, the open, cloudless sky; around us, the fresh breeze infused with the scent of wet grass and wood and overgrown greenery, alive with the chirp and hum of katydids and crickets; below us, the cold water.

Lucas paddled onward intensely. I followed at first, trying to keep pace, then slowed down and let my paddle rest on the kayak. I leaned back and let it glide on its own as I gazed up at the pure blue sky above, the egrets and sparrows soaring overhead.

"You all right back there?" Lucas shouted over his shoulder from twenty feet upstream.

"I sure am," I called.

He turned more completely and smiled. "I thought you might like this."

He paddled on again, and I watched as my kayak glided, unabated, through the water like scissor blades slicing through silk. Slowly, I dipped my paddle in, let it plunk into the water, then I pulled it out with subtle force and let it roll up out of the water again as its other end slid in. I felt completely in control, at one with the paddle, the kayak, the river.

It was like a dream I'd once had—of floating downstream in a boat, with a little man perched on the end, and I with no paddle. *Is this it?* I wondered. *Is this that dream, coming true? Where was that man leading me?*

I dismissed the thought, closed my eyes, and continued

159

rowing, freeing my grip so the current could do more of the guiding. "Let the river speak to you," the old man we rented kayaks from had said earlier. Lucas had grinned at me with raised eyebrows, as if to say "What a quack," but I loved the sound of those words. What was the river now trying to tell me? How consciously should I listen?

And how about if I resisted? How about if I kept that paddle under water, refused to let it reemerge?

I tried it and watched the paddle cut the stream, creating a ripple; my kayak swayed from left to right, edging closer and closer toward the water, until a complete and sudden loss of stability flipped me in with a thick splash.

My body hit the cold with the sharpness of a wine glass falling on a concrete floor—the same semirelief of shatter and shard. My feet remained in the kayak as I tried to grip the edges, but the river kept flowing onward, as it does, and I did, too; my head submerged beneath. I held my breath, flailed my arms. An eternity seemed to pass before I finally kicked myself free of the kayak and twisted my body enough for my fingertips to touch the open air, and then the rest of my body followed.

"Lucas!" I called. "Lucas!"

"Hang on, Rinie!"

"I can't hang on! There's nothing to hang onto!" My kayak flowed downstream.

"Just lift your toes up out of the water. Let the life jacket carry you!"

"I can't!"

"You can!" He paddled against the current toward me. When he reached me, he told me to grab onto the back of his boat and catch my breath. As I did, he placed one hand on my head, while the other held on to my kayak.

"You have my boat," I said, and I winced.

He smiled. "I do. Listen, you're okay. You just got scared,

160

but you're okay." He brushed the side of my face with the backs of his fingers. "You know, these aren't exactly rapids," he added with a laugh.

Safely back on land, we turned in our kayaks at the shop, to the same elderly gentleman with the graying beard and muddied pants rolled up to his knees who we rented them from earlier. "You're all wet," he said to me as we entered the store.

"I fell out of my boat," I explained.

"That right?" the old man yelped.

I nodded and stared at the man, who looked eerily like my Pappou. "It was weird," I said. "I kept my paddle in the water, thinking I could control my boat better, but it flipped me out."

The man clicked his tongue. "Not weird. It's like life, darlin'. God gives you an oar. He wants you to row your own boat. If you don't use it at all, you'll hit an obstacle, and you'll capsize. But if you dip your oar in too hard and try to leave it there . . . you'll capsize!" He let out a loud laugh. "Know what I'm sayin'?"

I did, and even though he couldn't have sounded any more different, I stared into his face to try to see if he was, in fact, somehow, my Pappou there, in spirit.

Lucas turned to me with that same look he gave me when the guy said, "Listen to the river." "What a trip, man," he said.

The old man burst into laughter. "A trip indeed." He gripped Lucas's shoulder. "You take care of this girl."

Each word—"You take care of this girl"—came out in a sizzling drip.

But I recoiled at the thought. I didn't need a man to take care of me. I hated the fact that I'd needed Lucas to come to my rescue there in the water, but more than that, I hated how relieved I felt when he did.

The old man nodded at me and pointed to Lucas. "And you take care 'a him, too, you hear?"

On our way home that night, we stopped at an Italian restaurant for dinner. It was housed in an old train car, dark and quaint, our booth tucked into a nook that blocked out all sight of anyone else in the place, our table lit by a small yellow candle.

"Your hair," Lucas said with a grin.

I touched my head and felt my hair, frizzed up high and wild into curls, and I smiled, tossing it back. "I like it like this. *Au naturel.*"

He smirked. "Me too."

I'd never felt so hungry in all my life. From the first sip of red wine, my neck burned, and my body slid into a deep mellow. I ate every bite of my dish, savoring each flavor—garlic, oregano, bay leaf, sage—the taste of each distinct.

We ate in silence. When the dishes were cleared, I reached for his hand, looked at the spot of Vodka sauce above his lip, and I laughed through tears I couldn't restrain.

"What's wrong?" he said.

I wiped my eyes. "Nothing."

There are a few reasons why I know this is Grandma's doing, one of which is that being around Lucas makes me feel, sometimes, the way I felt around her. Like I can say or do anything, and it doesn't have to mean something—I'm not being analyzed at all.

He doesn't always do the gentlemanly thing. He walks in front of me on the street, bumps into my shoulder and spills some of his drink on me without noticing, forgets to introduce me until five minutes into a conversation with an acquaintance.

But when he looks at me, I know that he sees me.

Lucas dropped me off the night of the kayak trip around 11 p.m. Eugenia was awake, watching television on the couch, while Salim slept soundly beside her.

"How was your day?" she asked, muting the television.

"How was my day? Where do I begin?" I plopped into an armchair. "Let's see, I almost drowned."

"What?" She sat up, and Salim snorted in his sleep.

"Well, I *felt* like I almost drowned."

Eugenia nodded.

"But it wasn't a big deal. I just fell out of my boat. Other than that, it was an amazing day. I don't know, it's like the whole world is different out there in the mountains. The sun is brighter, every color is more defined, and everything, every leaf, has this sharp outline against everything else. You can spend a half hour looking at one tree."

Eugenia laughed and rolled her eyes. "The leaves and the trees aren't any different out there, Rinie. You're just in love."

It zapped me to hear those words, "in love"—a phrase I never, *ever,* associated with myself. It made me think of being in a kind of lost-in-it state, something I didn't think I was, or didn't want to be, capable of.

"No." I shook my head and straightened my back. "It's just beautiful, nature."

That night, alone in my bedroom, after plugging my cell phone into its charger, I saw that I had a voicemail.

"Rinie." A shaky voice was on the other end. "It's Steve."

163

I hadn't heard from him in months, not since I'd told him about Lucas.

"I fucking hate you," he spat, and it was clear that he was drunk. "I fucking love you, but I fucking hate you. You left me. You've found someone new now and you don't need me any-more. But don't feel bad, because you can make it up to me. I want you to dig into that box you keep under your bed—yes, I know about that box—and find the letter I sent you on Octo-ber sixteenth of this year. It's dated, and it's like five pages long. I go on and on about how much you mean to me, how great I think you are, blah blah blah. Well, write down this code." He read off a long string of numbers. "Go through each word in the first paragraph and circle the letter in each word that corre-sponds with each number in the code. I know you're gonna get all *confused* and not know what I'm *saying*, so let me be clear: Since the first number is three, circle the third letter in the first word. And so on. I won't tell you why, just do it." He paused. "Goodbye, Irinie," he sang, and he clicked off the phone.

I followed his instructions, circling all the letters he asked me to circle. I assumed they'd form a phrase or sentence, but it seemed like gibberish. I wrote the sentence out on the bottom of the letter and stared at it, until I realized I was supposed to read it backwards: "Deb ni taer gerasl rig keerg," was actually supposed to read, "Greek girls are great in bed."

And now is the time for decision. Lucas and I are on a bench in Boston Common, enjoying the silence of early morn-ing before we head off to work for the day. I am sipping green tea, he a caramel-flavored latte. His arm is around me and we're staring out at the duck pond, at the swans on the water, the trees draping down, the mothers pushing strollers, the couples holding hands, the colors of life gentle and embalming. A Seurat painting come to life.

"I need to know," Lucas says. "I need to know what you decided." I can hear in his voice that it's taken something out of him to say this.

I pick at the seams of my green pleated skirt. "I want you to know that I really love . . . being with you," I say.

He doesn't look at me. "Just say it, Rinie."

"I'm going to Greece."

He looks down at his lap and pinches the corners of his eyes with his thumb and forefinger. This is when I realize how much he actually cares, how unambivalent he is about this decision.

"I really don't want to hurt you," I say. "I care about you so much. I just . . ."

"You just want to leave it all behind."

I glance to the right, at a roasted peanut stand, where a middle-aged man in a white apron is setting up shop for the day. "I just feel like I need to. I mean, I never wanted to be the type of person whose world revolves around a man. Who makes all her decisions for a man."

"Ouch."

"I don't mean it as bad as it sounds. It's not personal. It's not *you*. It's just . . ."

He laughs thinly. "It's not you, it's me."

"I'm serious. It *is* me. I still need to . . . find myself. And if it's meant to be, then we'll be together, and my leaving won't get in the way of that. It's like I need to do this for women everywhere." I sigh. "To live by my principles."

Lucas sits silent for a moment, staring at a pair of birds poised on the pavement, wildly flapping their wings at one another. "Rinie, life is not a concept. You can't just think your way through it all the time. Aren't you happy with me here? Don't you trust me yet?"

I bite my lip and squint. "It's not . . . that. It's . . ."

"Don't you freaking *want* to be happy?" He's standing now and pacing in front of the bench. "I mean, what the fuck?"

I've buried my face in my hands now. Part of me wants to say, "Never mind! Forget it, I'm staying here. Just kidding, I'm staying here." But there doesn't seem to be any turning back from a decision like this. So I simply say, "I'm sorry."

He puts a knuckle to his nose, covering his mouth as if to hold words back. "I don't know why I'm surprised. You've been pushing me away since the day I met you." He sits now and looks straight at me. "Listen, I actually love you. I actually want to be with you. But you say you need to find yourself, fig-ure out who you are? That's fine. There aren't any magic words I can tell you that will make the right buttons click in that head of yours, to make you feel safe with me." He laughs a little. "Believe me, I've tried." He sighs and gazes upward. "So go. Do what you gotta do. I can't say 'I'll wait for you' or any crap like that, because I don't know what the future holds." He shrugs and adds, sounding hopeless, "Like you said, I guess. If it's meant to be."

A cool breeze whips past, chilling me down to the bones, and I rub my bare arms with both hands, wondering if I'll ever feel warm again.

Chapter Twelve
Age Twenty-Two: A Winter in Greece

A panorama of memory: a name for that feeling of life as it flashes before your eyes.

It happened to me once on a middle-school snowboarding trip. I hit a bump and flew into the air, then slid straight off the trail and down the mountainside. Airborne, flipping, in that concentrated moment, I saw images in streams: my mother slicing cucumbers by the sink, glowing beneath the ceiling lamplight, handing a sliver to me without need for a glance in my direction. Vicky fastening the Velcro on my pink Barbie sneakers, the crackle of the strap, the feel of her tenderly tapping my toes as she completed the task. Eugenia and I riding our Cabbage Patch Kids tricycles down the hill in our backyard, the wind whipping in our faces. Mark wheeling my overalled-self around the yard in a barrow.

I've been reading about the concept in a book I bought from an English-language bookstore in Athens, that first weekend after I arrived here in Greece. What scientists say is that our perception of time is distorted in these moments; that fear causes it to slow, like tar choking the cogs in our minds. The memories are a survival instinct, the search for a solution to the problem at hand, a response to the threat of impending death or destruction. The Bible says it's an impetus to go back toward the light, to our lives. It's a moment of judgment—by God, or ourselves.

The theories faction off.

In any case, that wave—those bursts and blasts of memory—that's how it's felt here, these months I've spent in Greece: like one moment stretched wide, and colored in with snapshots of my past experience. I'll be on the bus or in a coffee shop and a moment will appear, so real, as if it were a hologram presenting itself to me; as if time itself were on a smoke break.

I'm working in a grocery store in town, in a dusty little market where I spend much of my day stooped on a stool shucking corn and trimming the ends off of string beans—services we perform for our customers. I savor these tasks, the smooth skin of the bean, the quick snap of the end revealing flesh. Foot traffic through the store these days is light; the island itself is eerily vacant. Mr. Kalogeros, the owner—an old friend of my Pappou's—asks me to rearrange the shelves each day to make them look full. We keep the lights in the back near the coolers turned off, to save on electricity. The store has a constant feeling of dusk. It's nothing like the megastores back home with their abrasive fluorescence, their suffocated products creating an illusion of limitlessness, infinity. Here, you can see behind and around each item on the shelf. Like the three lonely boxes of Corn Flakes that may or may not sell by winter's end.

The other day, while I was stuffing a can of tomato paste into a paper bag for an elderly woman, one of these visions came to me, so real, as if I were reliving it right there in the store. It was a Saturday morning, breakfast time. I was eight years old and had just finished my morning waffle. My siblings and I went outside to play. I climbed to the top of the grassy hill in our backyard, threw myself onto the ground, and then tumbled down the incline, my body rolling over bumps and dips as I laughed so hard there were tears streaming down and caking my face with dirt. Mark stood at the foot of the hill, cheering me on, and right there in the store where I stood behind the register, I could smell the fresh-cut lawn, feel it soft and cool against my skin. The sun was searing, a white-hot disc with rays sloping down like playground slides from Heaven.

"My child, how am I supposed to carry this heavy bag?" the lady barked, in the way these old ladies can—with affectionate familiarity and reproach—and the moment vanished. All I smelled was the dust in the store. All I felt was the nylon of my apron and the chilly air of the under-heated store.

That's pretty much how it goes.

Yiayia and I drink tea most nights on the veranda after supper. We wrap ourselves in afghans, woven by her own hands, to shield us from the evening winds, and she sits there like a lady in her powder-blue housedress, her feet crossed neatly at the ankles, while I hug my sweatpanted knees to my chest. I read or write in my journal, and she knits, looking up every once in a while to ask, "What are you writing in there?" or "What is it you're reading? What is in those books?" I respond with something like "ideas," if I'm writing in my journal, or "poems," if I'm reading a book of poems, or "a story," if I'm reading a novel, because I don't have the words to explain in more depth. She smiles and nods and will ask me the same questions again the following evening, because it's not really an answer she wants. "*Se kamarono,*" she tells me—"I'm admiring you."

Sometimes she tells me stories, of the village and what it was like back when all the men were away on the boats. How the women danced and cooked and feasted every Sunday. How they banded together to help each other raise their children, while their husbands sailed off for months or even years at a time. How they hid together beneath each other's kitchen tables while the Germans bombed the island during World War II.

How, as a little girl in that very house where we slept, she and her seven older brothers went days without eating anything more than the almonds and figs that grew from the nearby trees.

She tells me these stories with a smile, with the fondness of survival. It pains me to think of all the stories still entombed within her. Pains me to think of the day when I won't be able to hear them, at least not on this earthly plane. It pains me to the point where I almost want to end this pleasure, this pure and simple comfort of being beside her, because the thought of losing this is just too much.

But I'm starting to feel braver about these things. It has something to do, I think, with this distortion of time I've been experiencing here, the way I know and trust that moments like these can spread much wider than an ordinary, empty beat of time. They can return, unexpectedly, out of nowhere; they never, in this sense, actually end.

I like to imagine, too, that it's helping her, my listening, though I know the real benefit is to me.

Flashes of memory are common on these nights—a blip, a quick look: Yiayia at the ironing board, and myself as a young child, the crown of my head just grazing the bottom. I look up at her and she is glowing bright, and I say, "Yiayia, I need something to drink."

"*Portokalada,* my sweet?" This, she knows, is what I hoped for her to say. I can smell her spicy perfume, see her stringy black hair tousled on top of her head, her body tall and thin but strong, bent softly at the back, like an almost-bare tree in early spring. She folds up the ironing board and glides into the kitchen, where she stirs the sugary orange concentrate and mixes it with water. I accept the glass from her hand and gulps down all the liquid at once. She smiles and says, "*Bravo!* This will make you strong." And I already feel that I am.

170

There's a woman in town I paint with once a week. Her name is Polixeni, and my guess is that she's just about my mom's age. I met her one day in late September at the bus stop while I was outbound, heading back to Yiayia's after work, and she was traveling in from the port where she'd gotten off the ferry from Athens.

I was sitting alone on a bench in the empty parking lot, amid a row of buses left mostly dormant for the winter months, listening to music through my headphones and struggling to read a Greek fashion magazine, when she walked right up and said, "Who are you?"

I said nothing in return because I was too busy wondering if she were a mirage. She was the only person in sight and wore a drapey, flowy dress with purple, black, and magenta bands. Her eyelids were painted into a rainbow with shadow. I wondered how she found the space for each layer of color; where she found the faith to believe there would be enough.

She smiled a deep, penetrating smile, her whole face involved—not magnified or brightly lit, but dimmed into a soft, steady gleam. Her voice was breathy and low, yet melodious—distinctly feminine. "Your name, my dear."

"I'm . . . my name is Irinie."

"And the family name?"

"Pothos. Irinie Pothos."

She waved her scarf theatrically across her chest to her back. "What a name!" she shouted. "Peace and desire. You poor child. You know, one cannot experience the former if she hasn't reckoned with the latter." Her head rolled back and she gazed at the sky, then again at me. "And what are you doing here, Irinie Pothos?" Her shoulders lifted as she spoke my name, and she sniffed the pleasant air.

I told her that I worked at Mr. Kalogeros's store and was going home for the day. Her next question, "Where is home?" The village of Rafti, my Yiayia's house—these did not satisfy her as answers.

"My dear, it seems clear to me that there is much more for us to say," she said. "We must not allow this to be the last time we speak." She handed me a business card, which itself seemed out of place in this little island town. Beneath her name, "Polixeni Harambou," were two addresses: an Athenian one, on the Avenue Alexandras, and another one that simply read, "Café del Mar, Minos." She pointed to the second one and said, "You'll come see me here this week. Tuesday afternoon."

She nodded, and so I did, too.

There are darker nights as well out on my grandmother's porch. Last month, when Yiayia had gone off to Athens to visit Thia Mina, I stayed home alone. The island air is clammy and cold these days, nothing like the blazing summer heat I'd always enjoyed as a child. The plants are dying off, and the stillness, the silence, is heavy with the weight of time and lives past, with all the lives and the love and war that has come and gone through the village. That night, I stared into the darkness of the stone path that led up to the house, and I saw a parade of faces—Agnes, Andy, Sarah Mitchell, Steve, Jack, Tyler; even Richard Bosch. And I thought of Mark—his face bloodied, his body alone, limp, dead in a car. And myself, just staring. Helpless.

That night I had a nightmare so real it seemed my waking was the dream. In it, I'd been hiding in Calypso's stable, just as I did on the last day I saw Pappou alive. I clutched to my chest, in the dream, a pink stuffed bunny, soft with floppy ears. Pappou stalked over, seeming ten feet tall above me. He reached down and grabbed the toy from my hands and tore it apart, threw its pieces to the ground, and shouted, "So this? This is what you think I am? This is how you remember me?"

I woke with a sharp pain on the top of my hand and saw three lines of crimson blood, not oozing, just freshly caked there on my skin. I glanced around the room for a sign of him, his ghost. I heard the bleat of a goat outside my window and wondered if he, the goat, had been involved somehow in this blood. And the dream. Did it mean that Pappou had seen something rotten in me after all? Something cold and unlovable?

The last time I'd seen him alive, I was fourteen. When he died the following year, I didn't go to the funeral. From thousands of miles away in America, it was easy to forget that he wasn't still alive, waking up early every morning to feed the animals, napping in the afternoons, drinking Ouzo in the evening on the veranda. He remained alive in my mind until that next summer, when we returned to find Calypso's stable empty (she'd hung herself after his death), his twin bed untouched, his coffee flask still set beside the sink in the house where Yiayia, who seemed to have aged ten years, was living alone for the first time. But by then, it was too late for the type of tears that could wash away overwhelming emotion. Any pain had hardened, impossible to drain.

As I stared at the gashes on my hand, I thought about him, about how I'd never said goodbye; about how I believed for years that he had lost his faith in me. Was this his spirit tearing at the skin of my hands as punishment for my doubt?

It took me some time—weeks—to realize that it had been my own fingernails, and mind, doing the damage.

Polixeni paints in a studio above Café del Mar, which is owned by a close friend of hers. She lives and works in the studio during the fall and winter months. When I asked her why she avoided the vibrant summers, she told me, "I enjoy the lingering memory of life, the haunting, more than the actual experience. This is a reality of mine that I have accepted over the years and embraced."

She always has an answer like that, and it's interesting to hear her speak. She knows I'm here looking for my own purpose, trying to figure out how to be of most use to the universe—trying to figure out whether or not it's even worth trying to do so—but she won't volley an opinion. She simply tells me to paint. So we do, on Tuesday nights. We begin around five, she insists, so we can use the remaining bits of daylight and move together, in our work, into the darkness. Everything she does is determined with intention.

The first day in her studio, she set me up with an easel near an expansive window facing the ocean. At first I struggled to begin. I remembered the paintings I'd created while taking my art class in college. A muddled portrait or landscape that closed in on itself would disgust me to the point where I would launch it down eleven flights through the garbage shoot. I'd stand there and listen to the clang with an awful mix of pleasure and loss.

But Poli tells me not to worry, and now I don't. She says painting is about pleasure, and pleasure is *important,* and there's something about the way she says it that makes me believe her. Working in her studio on that first painting—which was nothing more than a teal and purple sky—I was staring out at the ocean, the cold winter waves crashing down on a deserted shore, when I saw a vision of my nursery school graduation. My young self holding up a diorama that my mother helped me make. We had cut fish patterns from orange construction paper and hung them from the top of a shoe box with yellow yarn, painted the inside of the box blue for the sea and green for the

174

algae, and wrapped it in a turquoise cellophane. I wore a navy-blue skirt with tiny red flowers lining the seams. Pink felt hearts dotted my stockings, which bunched around the ankles. In the image, I am beaming, proud of our work. My father holds a camcorder, Vicky wields a Fisher Price camera, Eugenia is kneeling and smiling at me from the front row, and Mark is standing by the entrance with a simple pink rose in his hand.

I asked Polixeni one day why she does this for me; why she offers me this time and space. She said she likes the company of fresh youth, of fresh energy. She says she has plenty of room and supplies and, for that matter, money, and I am no bother. "Besides, you've got something to say. And I'm waiting for you to begin to say it." That makes me feel a kind of pressure, which I realize is not going to help me achieve her goal.

She's got tattoos that run up her forearms—one is of a Hindu goddess named Saraswati, who is dressed in all gold and wears a dome-shaped crown. She is the goddess of knowledge and the arts, Poli says; she is the *Shakti,* or power, of Brahma, who is the Hindu god of creation. Her name means something like "she who has flow," because she is connected in some way to water. She's also the creation part of a trinity—the Hindu apparently have one, too—that also includes both maintenance and destruction.

These concepts are mesmerizing to me; sometimes, I put my brush down, sit on my stool, and just watch while she speaks and paints. One of my favorite of Poli's tattoos is of an ebony-skinned beauty in a simple red dress named Oya, a Yoruban goddess of the wind and storms. "What I destroy you no longer need," is her motto, which is inscribed in Greek beneath the image on Poli's skin.

In the past, these tattoos might have made me feel nervous, disoriented. I'd have wondered what it all meant—that Saraswati is the power behind the male god of creation; that his power is actually a woman and also water, and that she is linked to both maintenance and destruction: two poles at seeming odds with one another, yet linked by this figure, this force that can go either way. And yet, there's Oya, who destroys what we no longer need.

I would have wondered, in the past, if it were wrong or right to adorn one's skin with such images. What kind of trouble might that court?

But I've gotten to know Polixeni now, and I can see that these images are something she needs. She's a strong woman, but that may be, in part, because she keeps these images close to her, and maintains her patterns: Minos to paint in the cold, and Athens to explore in the heat. These tattoos are a reminder—of what, I'm not exactly sure. She doesn't share the details of her life, her past, but I can tell that these are a part of it, or an outgrowth. So if these tattoos keep her grounded and sane; if they bring her peace—enough to reach out to someone like me, and help me in all the ways she's already helped me—how could anyone—how could God—disapprove?

But even this, my unformed confusion, she picks up on. "You're surprised by my tattoos," she said one night, without from her canvas. "You thought maybe I would just have Greek goddesses here on my arms? Maybe a cross? You are surprised by the African, Hindu?"

I had to admit that I was. Not because they weren't lovely, but because where I came from, Greeks were just so proud to be Greek. For them, it was a way to hold onto something they'd lost. I guess that's not so unlike what Poli is doing.

"We are human animals," she said, her voice stretching out the words like kneaded dough, her eyes still set on her work. "That is our fate—we feel pain, in our bodies, our spirits, but also our minds. That is our blessing and curse. We have questions, and we seek answers, knowing—if we are thoughtful—

176

that the answers themselves are only questions. No single set of people can hold them. There is wisdom to be found everywhere, or else nowhere. We must not stop seeking." Her voice remained steady and low, as if she were reciting a poem. "I love this country, this land, and its people, too. But I am so much more, as a human animal, than just 'Greek.'"

I thought about Grandma, her last words: *You're not just Greek; don't be like me.* It had been a warning: that it's good to be good, but it's not good to lose your mind. Not good to lose yourself.

"I do have this, though," Poli added. She turned and pulled down on the back of her dress to reveal an image on her upper torso. It was of Asteria, the Greek goddess of the stars, who said *no* to Zeus's advances, and then harbored other women who escaped him. "This is not something I need to see myself. At least not anymore. This is for those behind me."

I don't communicate much with home. My parents call every once in a while and ask when I'm coming back. I say I'm not ready, not yet. My father says, "We miss you." My mother says, "Don't get stuck there." They mean well. But, naturally, they want to know what I will do with my degree, with my life.

I talked to Vicky for a while one day. When I told her I was doing well, she said, "You sound like you really mean that."

"I do," I told her. "Why wouldn't I?"

She said I had seemed so mixed up before I left, not as much of a mess as the year before, but still confused. "We were all so worried about you," she said.

I hadn't been as invisible as I thought. Or hoped.

Eugenia asked me one day if I'd heard from Lucas. The question singed, because I hadn't. I'd written him a letter back in October, asking him how he was doing and letting him know how things were going here. Now, in December, I still haven't heard back. I've rationalized that the island's postal service is rather slow. And yet, a letter from Steve eked through. It was an apology, which I swiftly accepted. I'd hurt him, without meaning to, and he hurt me in return, which wasn't the way to act—and I told him that, in my reply—but I understood. The apology I'd really wanted—from Andy; something more than simply a cursory morning-after acknowledgement; a true recognition of what had been violated—was never coming. I knew that. And it didn't matter anyway, because—all along—it was myself I've had the harder time forgiving.

I've learned that here in time.

I told Eugenia that, no, I hadn't heard from Lucas, and it felt strange to say his name aloud; I hadn't done so in months. I can barely allow myself to think of him these days.

She told me she'd met him for coffee about a month ago. She said he missed me.

"How can you tell? Does he seem mad at me?" I asked.

"To be honest, yeah, a little," she said. "But I tried to explain . . . how you get scared of things."

"What do you mean?"

"You know what I mean," she said, and it was true that I did.

On the anniversary of Pappou's death, Yiayia and I took a trip to Tinos, a neighboring island that houses a holy church, Panagia Evangelistria, believed to be the site of miracles.

It also fell on a major Greek Orthodox feast day, and so Yiayia had many friends heading there, too. But on the boat ride over, she just waved to them from a distance, dismissing the expectancy in their faces, and we sat out on the deck in silence. She held her purse close to her belly like a pillow and stared out at the waves. This was unusual; she liked to socialize, to laugh. She ordinarily remained happily conscious of the presence of others beside her. I got the sense that this uncharacteristic silence was part of a ritual for her, a veneration of the day and its magnitude.

Later, I watched her during the service. As the priest read her husband's name, Alexandros, among the many others of those deceased, she did not shed one tear, though it was clear from the way she gripped the oak of the pew, her lips tightly pursed, her gaze fixed toward the altar, that she missed him, still, with an awe-provoking intensity. As the priest chanted "Memory everlasting" and swung the censer back and forth, wafting the oaky scent of frankincense and a thin cloud of smoke throughout the church, she gestured the sign of the cross in rhythm, as if the motion itself were a soulful "Amen."

After the service, we had lunch with the ladies, her friends, at a tavern near the port. She returned to her usual, charming self—laughing, joking, reveling in the company, exuding her mirth. But part of her, I could see, was still in that place, in that church, in that service, paying devotion to her husband's memory, and I admired that ability to remain so present in both places.

When the meal was over, she rose and said, "Goodbye, ladies."

"You're leaving?" they said. "Stay! We'll board the ship together!"

She raised a hand in protest. "No, I am with my granddaughter. It will be the two of us."

We sat inside the cabin on the boat ride home, in facing armchairs beside a large window. I felt full, not just from lunch but from the heft of the day. The fullness gave me a sense of urgency and impatience, a need for something I couldn't pin-point.

"Yiayia," I said. "You and Pappou married young, didn't you?"

Her eyes softened, and she sighed. "I was sixteen."

"And did you love him?"

"Did I love him!" She placed a hand on her heart and sat forward. "My child, my love for him has been the defining fea-ture of my life." She sighed again. "But of course, I didn't love him at first. I didn't even know what love *was*."

"And what is it?" I said.

"Hoh!" She clapped her hands together, then flipped them apart. "What do I know? All I know is that I thank God every day that I have it."

The boat rocked deeper to the left and right, and I wrapped my arms around the sides of the chair. Yiayia looked at me generously, offering more, so I asked, "But how did you know you could trust him, all those years he spent on the boats and in America?"

She leaned toward me and put a hand on my knee. "Well, one thing I do know, my dear, is that trust—whatever that is— is the same *thing* as love. Don't get me wrong, though, my child. It's not that I had any illusions about your Pappou being per-fect. I'm sure there were times when he . . . made mistakes of all kinds. But who doesn't? That is life. That is what it means to be a person. What I'm saying is something else. I *chose* to love him. And myself. Every day I chose, and I still do."

We withdrew into silence again for a few moments. Out-side, night was falling, the last bit of pink on the waves nearly faded to black. "Tell me," I said after a while. "Tell me, Yiayia. What should I do with my life?" I was surprised to hear my own words, so frank and simple, but I felt a desperation, a sense that it was now or never.

She turned her thin face toward me and set her smoky black eyes, sunken deep into leathery skin, onto mine. "When your father was a little boy, he had no fear. *No fear.* He would leap from balconies, swim far into the ocean, ride his bicycle with no hands down steep hills. There was so much love and trust in his heart, he believed he could do anything. The ladies in the village, they told me, 'Your boy, he is too wild. He will not survive.' But I knew they were wrong. I feared they were right, but I knew they were wrong. I prayed for him every day, and I asked the other ladies in the village to pray for him, too. And I came to Tinos, like we did today, and I prayed for him there. That's what I believed. And you know what? He did survive. And he had you kids." She paused and peered out the window. "He learned something. I don't know what, and I don't know how. Your mother? The business? America? You kids? Something taught him how to be fearless and also survive." She turned to face me again. "Me, I knew fearlessness, too—my child, he got it from me—but I didn't know how to keep hold of it. Women, we didn't know such things then."

I wanted to pluck each word she spoke from the air and preserve it somehow, sanctify and store it for future use. I nodded in hopes that she'd continue.

"But you? This is a different time. You have it in you, too, but I can see, you are burying it beneath fear. What to do with your life, I don't know. Only you can know. But you don't, yet, and I pray to the good Lord that you will, and will do something." She smacked a hand on my bare thigh, then pinched my cheek. "Oh, I could just eat you up!" And she laughed, loud and free.

A few days after our trip to Tinos, on a day off from the shop, I awoke early, packed a bag with fruit and water, and told

Yiayia that I would be gone for the day, that I had somewhere to be. I didn't tell her where, because I didn't want her to worry or demand to come along. I set out on a hike up the mountain across the way, to the monastery near the top, the one I'd gazed at and wondered about every summer as a little girl.

The hike took hours. As the air grew thin and colder, my head felt lighter. I concentrated on the endless rock and earth beneath my feet until I reached halfway up, where I rested for a bit and looked out across the valley, then behind me. Seeing how much more terrain I had left to travel, I wondered if I should turn back, but I decided to forge ahead, one step at a time.

When at last I reached the top, I walked to the front gate of the church, but when I tried the handle, I found it locked. The place seemed deserted. "Of course," I said to no one.

I trekked around the outer walls and found a boulder on the mountainside, where I decided to perch and rest. There, I sat and stared across at the opposite mountain, at our village. From this distance, all the houses appeared like pushpins on a bulletin board, tiny white dots surrounded by a vast expanse of green and brown. How small it was, and yet so large in my mind.

The wind blew strong, and I stooped to my knees, closed my eyes, let it toss my hair across my face. I cast my arms out to my sides, palms up, and pushed against it. I thought of Yiayia, how far below she was, preparing a feast for just the two of us. How much it meant to her, the ritual of food. I thought of my mom, the way she used to clip magazine articles for us with advice on how to find your true calling, or what colors to wear to feel happier. I thought of each one of my family members, as if I could suddenly see into their souls, past their deepest fears, into the thing that made them feel safe and alive.

Maybe I should stay up here forever, I thought. *Maybe this is where I'd do the most good.*

I sat there for an hour, until I knew Yiayia might begin to worry. On the way back down, I took a different route, through the valley by the bridge that crossed the river where I nearly drowned so many years before. I sat on a stone with my feet dangling down, and remembered—Pappou, holding me in his arms while I shivered in wet clothes. How he carried me back to the house and handed me off to Yiayia, who blessed me with oils, ridding me of the *muti.*

Who was it that saved me that day? Was it Pappou, who found and carried me? Or was it Yiayia, with her prayers and rituals? Had it been the both of them together? Or neither? Perhaps I hadn't been saved at all.

A strong wind blew by, yet I felt steadied by it. I looked up: a white pigeon flew overhead, beneath the cloudless sky. It swooped down before sailing up and out of sight.

I glanced at the water below—calm, benign—and saw a vision of Lucas and me at a jazz club we went to a few weeks before I moved. Every note an unexpected thrill, an inside joke we were both in on, the messy harmony like ocean waves parting and becoming one, parting and becoming one, undulating into one another and toward us and away, and toward us and away. In the vision, I felt triumphant, free, and *happy*—all the things you want to feel. I turned and looked at Lucas, who wrapped his arms around me and lifted me off the floor, and I was warmed, body and soul.

Then, something else happened. I saw myself as if I were not myself. What people call an "out of body experience"—another response to the threat of danger.

A little girl, awake in her bed, tortured by relentless

183

thoughts. An older girl, feeling ugly and alone. A young woman clinging too tightly to her innocence, which was slipping away slowly before disappearing all together. A woman who shut herself off from a source of healing. A girl—forever a girl—who missed her big brother. Who wanted him here. Who felt tired—of hiding, of longing, of fear. I saw her and felt sad for her. I wanted to help her. I wanted to trust her. Suddenly, I loved her.

I sat on that bridge, for minutes, an hour—I no longer had any sense of time passing. Vacant, yet at the same time infused with something essential, as if purging those tears had created room for everything else, all the sustenance I had forced this person, this self, to live without for too long.

That evening at dinner, I told my Yiayia that I was leaving.

"Good," she said. "It is time for you to return to your life."

At first I was surprised, but then not. I placed my palms on top of her hands and felt the brittle ridges of her bones through her soft, thin skin. I turned her hands over and held them, aware of their delicate weight, their fragile strength.

Later that night, moonlight shone on the dark and biting water. I plunged into the sea and coursed through the current, streaming parallel to a silent and distant shore.

Waking Slow
Reading Group/Teaching Guide

A note from the Author

I taught at the college level for about ten years, and attended college myself almost two decades ago, and in those years, I often felt baffled and caught unaware by so-called "campus culture." I expected college life to be predominated by intellectually-stimulating conversations about art, culture, politics, history, science—with, of course, some fun mixed in. What I found was that mindless "partying"—and everything that term encompassed—reigned supreme.

When I began writing this novel, I wanted to create a protagonist who was, perhaps, even more naive than I was: an outsider to the lifestyle—yet one who felt compelled or even obliged to actively enter and make sense of it. I wasn't aiming to create a spectacular story but, rather, to trace and examine the mundane absurdity and dehumanization that could be found within this context. Beyond that, I wanted to explore the widespread sexual assault and partner violence that we know is rampant on college campuses, and which is symptomatic of, perpetuated by, and continuously promulgating the endemic violence we see in society at large.

The types of violence this novel explores, beyond the initial assault, appear, on a micro level and might have been barely discernible if not for the heightened awareness and vulnerability of a protagonist such as Rinie, who is contending with untreated mental illness that has been exacerbated by the early loss of her brother, and the more recent loss of her grandmother. Yet this awareness allows Rinie to slowly awaken to the many injustices, indignities, and invalidations occurring ubiquitously around her.

This novel was written before Black Lives Matter and the #metoo movements made subjects of power and privilege daily mainstays in "mainstream" conversations and media. My hope is that it echoes the urgent need for these conversations to remain front and center—and to expand to include additionally marginalized and stigmatized groups—as we continue fighting to restore and improve our human culture.

Discussion Questions

1. How would you classify the genre of this novel? Coming-of-age? Spiritual quest? Something else?

2. What is the effect and purpose of the novel's structure, as it alternates between past and present?

3. How and why is Rinie's Greek-American identity important to this story?

4. To what extent, if at all, does Rinie have a moral obligation to report Andy's actions to campus authorities? Why does she choose not to, and what is the consequence of this choice?

5. Rinie is apparently dealing with untreated mental illness. Why doesn't she seek support or treatment? How typical do you think her experience is in this regard?

6. To what extent is Rinie a reliable narrator? How does her reliability affect or contribute to the story and its themes?

7. Rinie's story takes place before the age of social media. How might her experience play out differently today? What are the consistencies?

8. Is the ending of the novel satisfying, or does it feel too unresolved?

9. To what extent does Rinie undergo a transformation? If there were a sequel to this novel, what might happen?

Information and Resources

• One in five women and one in sixteen men have been sexually assaulted while in college.

• More than 90% of sexual assaults on college campuses go unreported.

Source: The National Sexual Violence Resource Center: https://www.nsvrc.org

• About 40 percent of college students reported difficulty functioning due to depression, while 61 percent cited having overwhelming anxiety in the past year, according to a 2017 survey by the American College Health Association (https://www.acha.org).

• Almost 73 percent of students diagnosed with a mental health condition experienced a mental health crisis on campus, while about 35 percent reported that their college did not know about their crisis, according to a 2012 survey report from the National Alliance on Mental Illness (https://www.nami.org).

About the Author

Ioanna Opidee lives in Connecticut with her husband and two daughters. She holds a BA from Boston College, an MA from the University of Massachusetts Boston, and an MFA from Fairfield University's Low Residency Program.

Ioanna has worked as a journalist for several publications including *Folio:* and *University Business* magazines. Her creative work has appeared in *Spry literary journal, Drunken Boat, Lumina, Talking Writing, Weave, Outside In,* and *The Huffington Post,* among other publications. She currently teaches at Weston High School in Connecticut and has previously taught at Fairfield University, the University of Connecticut Stamford, and the University of Massachusetts Boston.

For more information, please visit:www.ioannaopidee.com

(author photo: Neil Swanson)

Some Other Books by PFP / AJAR Contemporaries

a four-sided bed - Elizabeth Searle

A Russian Requiem - Roland Merullo

Ambassador of the Dead - Askold Melnyczuk

Big City Cat: My Life in Folk Rock - Steve Forbert

Blind Tongues - Sterling Watson

Celebrities in Disgrace (eBook version only) - Elizabeth Searle

Demons of the Blank Page - Roland Merullo

excerpt from Smedley's Secret Guide to World Literature
Askold Melnyczuk

Fighting Gravity - Peggy Rambach

"Gifted: An Indestructibles Christmas Story"-
Matthew Phillion

Girl to Girl: The Real Deal on Being A Girl Today-Anne Driscoll

"Last Call" (eBook "single") - Roland Merullo

Leaving Losapas - Roland Merullo

*Like A Come*t - Matthew Phillion

Lunch with Buddha - Roland Merullo

Make A Wish But Not For Money - Suzanne Strempek Shea

Music In and On the Air - Lloyd Schwartz

My Ground Trilogy - Joseph Torra

Passion for Golf: In Pursuit of the Innermost Game - Roland Merullo

Revere Beach Boulevard - Roland Merullo

Rinpoche's Remarkable Ten-Week Weight Loss Clinic -
Roland Merullo

Revere Beach Elegy: A Memoir of Home & Beyond - Roland Merullo

Taking the Kids to Italy - Roland Merullo

Talk Show - Jaime Clarke

Temporary Sojourner - Tony Eprile

the Book of Dreams - Craig Nova

Lunch with Buddha

"A beautifully written and compelling story about a man's search for meaning that earnestly and accessibly tackles some well-trodden but universal questions. . . . A quiet meditation on life, death, darkness and spirituality, sprinkled with humor, tenderness and stunning landscapes."

Made in the USA
Middletown, DE
26 March 2021